Tales for a Blue Moon

by

Jeff Guenther

Wyzard Hill Press

For information contact:
https://JGuentherAuthor.WordPress.com
Cover design by J Guenther. CC0 cover image.
CrimsonText-SemiBold.ttf: Copyright © 2010, Sebastian Kosch (sebastian@aldusleaf.org), with Reserved Font Name "Crimson".
IMFePIsc28P.ttf: © 2007 Igino Marini (www.iginomarini.com) With Reserved Font Name IM FELL DW Pica SC
Interior design by J Guenther, typeset in Times New Roman.
Printed in the United States of America
ISBN: 978-0-9974503-6-1
First Edition: November 2018
10 9 8 7 6 5 4 3 2 1

Also by J Guenther

Sail Away on My Silver Dream, 2019

In the Mouth of the Lion, 2016

A True Map of the City, 2019

Moon Over the Lost City, 2019

The Perils of Tenirax, 2019

Praise for Sail Away on My Silver Dream

A fanciful book that deals with some of today's real problems. I recommend it highly. A very enjoyable read. – Jean Shriver

This book is for anyone dealing with alcoholism, domestic violence and loss. Very realistic. – Mary Jo Hazard, MFT

Guenther's sensitive portrayal of two kids who find their way through difficult times by sailing to exotic, faraway places aboard their imaginary sailboat, the Silver Dream, is a story that will be enjoyed by young readers, and treasured by readers of all ages. – Dave Kenney.

Praise for In the Mouth of the Lion

An impressively original, exceptionally well written, and inherently fascinating novel, "In the Mouth of the Lion" is an extraordinarily entertaining read from cover to cover. – Midwest Review

"Overflowing with rich history… thorough and wildly entertaining… human nature in its cruelest form… engrossing in a way that history books rarely are… insightful… meticulous… a stunning novel… highly competent." –Self-Publishing Review

DEDICATIONS

To my teachers:

Gibson Reaves, Richard Condon, Dr. Julia McCorkle, Jeff Hoppenstand, Edith Battles, Anne Lowenkopf, Glad Esther Mitchell, Bill Barnett, Geri Howard.

TABLE OF CONTENTS

The Blessing of the Animals

Folks, this coming Sunday, October 4th, will be Schroon Lake Chapel's third annual "Feast of St. Francis Blessing of the Animals." There's a lot of interest again this year. We've already received twenty or thirty phone calls and a dozen anonymous notes shoved under the rectory door.

I'll try to allay your concerns. First off, I'm sure there will be no repeat of last year's problems. We've set some new guidelines, and if we all follow them, we probably won't need the paramedics again.

In answer to many questions, yes, we still encourage you to bring your animals two-by-two, just like Noah. We only ask that you use separate cages for animals of each . . . er . . . gender. We're going to have to insist on this. Miss Milligrew is still seeing a therapist since last year's elephant incident.

And while we're on the subject of elephants, Mr. Gupta, please leave your elephants at home next Sunday. You caught us by surprise last year. When we said, "bring your elephants," we were joking. We never dreamed that anyone in Schroon Lake had an actual elephant, let alone two of them. Yes, we know it wasn't your fault, Dildip. Please just bring photos to bless, this year. Yes, photo blessings are just as effective. And to be perfectly clear, bring a photo of each elephant, separately. Please don't bring any you took during last year's . . . incident. Amen. Thank you. Amen.

We regret having to say that monkeys are also in the photos-only category, now, unless they're confined in plastic-lined cages. I don't expect any objections to that decision. Yes, amen.

I'll personally bless all your pets or photos, as always. I'll ask, however, that any dog capable of biting higher than my knee be kept on a very, very tight leash. We're also going to insist that all dogs who participated in the free-for-all two years ago continue to wear muzzles at this year's service. You know who I mean. No muzzle, no blessing.

And we'd like to remind you that if pooches start howling in unison at any point during the service, parishioners are urged not to join in. It isn't helpful; it only gets our pets over-excited and makes the floor slippery.

And, speaking of slippery, Greg Beadleman has ordered a ton of sawdust delivered Saturday. We have ten volunteers to spread the sawdust in the chapel Saturday evening. So far, we don't have any people to sweep up the used sawdust after the service and wheel it over to the Josiah Poovey Memorial Compost Garden, in back of the rectory. Please see Greg to volunteer. Between the sawdust and the new snake policy, we should have no more domino-effect falls and injuries during the recessional.

Which brings me to the snake rule: Snakes, too, are now in the "photos only" category, whether caged or not. We still haven't found Mr. Locke's pit viper that somehow got loose last year. Relax, we're pretty sure it's dead. We looked for it everywhere. We even checked the bottoms of Mr. Gupta's elephants' feet. No luck. It was there in the cage for the blessing, but at the end of the service, Mr. Locke found the cage empty, just as we began our procession from the chapel.

Yes, you're right, *procession* isn't quite the word for what took place after Mr. Locke yelled, "My viper is loose!" Thank you again for that timely heads-up, Mr. Locke. Sorry for your loss. Your snake probably crawled away and died during Mabel Crowley's concluding solo. Er, let me make it clear I'm not suggesting that was cause and effect. Mabel's falsetto rendition of "All Things Bright and Beautiful" was just as . . . as incredible as ever. Let's have a round of applause for Mabel. Thank you.

Okay, we'll see you next Sunday for our Blessing of the Animals. Be sure to bring all your friends and relatives.

Arma Virumque Cano

"Hey! You!" the man said, waving a knife in his hairy fist.

Alarmed, Adolfo stared at the knife. The blade was not shiny, but spotty and dull with dried dishwater. Adolfo felt responsible for the dirty knife, though it was Sergio who washed the dishes at the *Lavender Flamingo*.

Table 34 held up the knife, glaring at Adolfo; Adolfo must be at fault. He was always at fault. His father had assured him of this many, many times.

"This knife is dirty!" Table 34 said. "It's covered with crud. You call this clean?"

Adolfo considered a reply. "Yes, sir," might sound like Adolfo did call the knife clean, which it clearly wasn't. "No, sir," might seem to deny that the knife was dirty, which it clearly was. This dilemma held Adolfo tongue-tied. Unable to think of a suitable reply, he could only reach beneath his white uniform jacket, pull out his parkerized automatic, and riddle Table 34 with .45 caliber slugs. Blam-Blam! Blam-Blam-Blam!

Blam-Blam! Adolfo pumped two more rounds into Table 34 to calm himself. Sweetly tart gun smoke arabesqued toward the Celotex ceiling. As Table 34 slumped forward, Adolfo remembered the right thing to say: "I'll get you another knife from the kitchen, sir," he said, plucking the offending utensil from the diner's limp fingers.

Adolfo inserted a fresh magazine, holstered the weapon and slipped away unobtrusively, hoping no one had been watching. He commandeered a fresh napkin roll from Table 42 and took cover behind a large fern. Unobserved, he extracted a clean knife, polished it with the napkin until it gleamed, then swabbed his sweaty brow before returning to Table 34.

Table 34 was reading the menu. He looked up and stared over his spectacles at Adolfo. Adolfo bowed and silently placed the sparkling knife near where the man's tweeded elbow wrinkled the linen. The man went back to the menu and said nothing. Adolfo said nothing. It seemed the safest course.

Adolfo cleared Tables 35, 38, and 41 and staggered toward the kitchen. Before he could reach that white-tiled sanctuary, Table 47 held up her cup, silently requesting more coffee. Coffee was Juan's job, but Juan was nowhere in sight. Adolfo thought he could handle it himself. Table 47 was not angry, so Adolfo was even able to speak. "Right away, madam," he said, rushing past.

He unburdened himself in the kitchen and dashed to the coffee station, where another dilemma immobilized him: Two pots of coffee: one old and murky, one fresh, with amber drops still bobbing about on the dark, steamy surface. The manager had ordered the staff to use up the old before pouring the fresh. Adolfo bent down and gauged the level of the old coffee, hoping it was too low to use. There was, alas, enough for a full cup.

The diner was waiting; a decision had to be made. Old coffee is muddy and bitter, but Adolfo had his orders. On the other hand, Table 47 was very pretty. Adolfo vacillated for long seconds, then grabbed up the fresh coffee, hurrying to make up for the time lost in indecision.

"I wanted decaf," Table 47 announced at the very moment the fresh, steaming coffee filled her cup to the brim. This wounded Adolfo. Another mistake, and now the blame was his alone. It was no good to point a finger at Sergio this time. He considered blaming Juan, forever slow to notice empty cups, but no, it was Adolfo who had poured the wrong coffee.

He felt too bad to apologize or say anything at all. He emptied the cup back into the carafe and slunk away, surreptitiously extracting the grenade from the left pocket of his jacket, pulling the pin with his teeth, and arcing the device over his right shoulder. He ran, head down, and ducked behind the coffee station a half second before the grenade exploded.

Metal fragments splintered Table 47 into the Celotex. Particle board dust rained like grated parmesan on all the silent diners. Tables 46 and 48 were also badly damaged, their shredded linen now hanging like lace.

As Adolfo surveyed the wreckage, Juan passed by, bearing fresh decaf in an orange carafe. "Thank you so much," Table 47 said, smiling, her eyes actually focused on Juan. Adolfo felt a pang of jealousy. He pulled out his .45 and aimed it two-handed at Juan. But no, it was truly not Juan's fault. Adolfo tucked the pistol back beneath his armpit, patted it, and reconnoitered the kitchen counter.

Table 22's *Veal Cutlet Special Du Jour* lay beneath a heat lamp, no longer sizzling, not even steaming. Reba's number shone accusingly overhead, unseen by anyone but Adolfo. It was also he alone who knew that Reba was out in the alley, inhaling white powder. Anxiety gripped him. He wanted to snatch up the plate and dash to Table 22 before the au gratin potatoes surrendered their faint, final warmth. But he was forbidden to do this. He went out back and semaphored silently, urgently to Reba in the filthy darkness.

Later, as he cleared Table 22, Adolfo's anxiety returned. At first, everything seemed to be there: the pepper, the salt, the flatware. The plastic flowers in their plastic vase, and the catsup, too. Everything sat where it was supposed to . . . except the tip. There was no tip on the table. A fourth of the tip was to be Adolfo's. A fourth to the bearer of beverages, Juan. Half to Reba of the runny nose. But there was nothing, nothing at all.

The diner formerly known as Table 22 still lingered at the register. Adolfo hoped he would return to cascade currency upon the table, or perhaps leave a substantial sum with the cashier. But, no, he merely ambled toward the door, counting his small change.

Adolfo zigzagged across the dining room and threw himself on the flowered carpet beside Table 4. He aimed and pulled the trigger of his M-16 once, twice. Bla-ham! Bla-ham! Twice the weapon squirmed in his hands, pounded his shoulder, slapped his eardrums. The figure in Adolfo's sights stopped, crumpled, and lay inert beside the gum ball machine. A nickel whirred round and round the vinyl entry flooring, loud in the silence of Adolfo's mind.

Reba slid up beside him as he stood watching the departing guest step out onto La Cienega Boulevard. "Didn't leave a tip, did he?" she said. Adolfo shook his head slowly. Reba touched his arm, consoling him: "He never does. He's a deadbeat. I remember him from IHOP. He used to try to skip on the check sometimes, too. Screw *him*."

She looked closely at Adolfo for the first time that evening. "Say, you don't look so hot, Adolfo. You look like you been in a war or something. You sure you don't wanna try a little coke, hon?"

He shook his head again. He needed to keep his wits about him if he was going to make it home safely. It was still early in the evening, and Adolfo was already out of grenades.

The Eight Times Cut Stone

The old language of our planet is dying. If you people stay here, it will soon pass away, and we will speak only your Anglic language. Tell me I am wrong! Raise your hand in dissent, *Hoo-man hreg-schulah* Doctor.

But you cannot. Fewer of us speak the old language every season-cycle. Over there, in the haircutter's, yestereve, a grey-haired person sat upon the cutting bench and greeted me in Anglic as I entered. I replied, *"con-drelbau'h,"* and he looked at me with head tilted, brows knotted. He simply didn't remember the meaning of *con-drelbau'h*, our ancient and common blessing for his hour.

If he had been a youngling, my heart-torn-outness would have been far less. A youngling might not have yet learned all of the Waytongue. But when elders lose the Waytongue, all shall lose it, for grey heads are the ultimate living repositories of our language and all else that makes us a true people.

What is the loss, you ask? Is not one word as good as another? The *Hoo-man hreg-schulah* doctor who came here before you understood. He was—what is your word?—a philologist, one who loves languages. He knew that words are much more than scrawlings on leaves or scratchings in clay or flutterings of the air beside your ears. He was sent home, I understand, because his presence here did not enhance sufficiently the *bottom line*, as your people say.

Yes, our language is dying, gradually replaced by glibly mercenary Anglic. With it fade the logic of our ways and our people-being. Our common Waytongue holds artifacts of our history, artifacts that your *company* can't dig up and sell to museums on your planet—Dirt, is it not called? Earth? Ah, I see the distinction. But do you see my point?

The Waytongue contains the *whys* and the *long agos*. You Hoo-mans have a word: *tradition:* something you people do for which you've forgotten the reason. Among you, traditions are soon forgotten, too! Nothing lasts. Nothing. The few traditions you have are dying.

Yes, I am right about this; I see dismay invade your eyes as I speak.

You are a mighty people, and you make clever, seductive things and marvelous works. But the people you are, they will not exist in a few great cycles. Oh, yes, descendants *may* exist, but they will not be of your people. Ah, Doctor! How your forehead strains to keep my thought from spilling back out of your head! I explain:

When your traditions fade, when your language and art decay, your descendants will have nothing in common with you. They will find all your works incomprehensible. The gulf between you and your progeny will exceed that between you and me today. Your great works, all you have done, all you have built, will be at best mere puzzles to your descendants.

One of our words for tradition is *zereb*. In Anglic, roughly, "remember-done-because." Appended words explain the *why*. An example: our tradition of leaving a new sword on an altar overnight. This is called *zereb-Las-zer'n*, "done because anciently Las did." To truly understand, you must know who Las was, something I shall not tell you today.

Our reasons are contained in our tradition-words, and our traditions survive. We do not easily abandon traditions, thus forgotten reasons never arise and bite us later. That is, before you *Hoo-man hreg-schulah* came here.

Another example? Let me find something with little subtlety, that you might understand. Ah, yes. See the paving here ahead of us, in front of our barter house? Observe this black stone. Be careful; don't step on it. That is permitted only to children, whose bare feet will not scratch it. That date reads "67733." In your system, that is season-cycle minus 27584. The inscription is worn, hard to read. In another few hundred cycles, someone will cut the numbers deeper. This has already happened seven times, and that fact is in the name of this stone. Yes, this stone has a name: *berel-dach-kanlui*. After the next incising, it will become *berel-dach-detlui*.

An important stone, to have a name, you think? But it is *not* important compared to those who have walked across it, and we honor their memory by preserving the stone exactly thus. My great-

great-great-grandfather stepped on that stone as a child and later stepped over it on the way to his workplace. I know this. As I walk over it, now, I think of him and all the others who have done so and will do so. My great-great-great-grandchildren will also walk over this stone, if you haven't dug it up and taken it away, too.

But my descendants, if there are any, may forget its name, its importance, and why not to step on it. In time, the date may wear completely away. No one will think to re-incise it. Perhaps it would be better if you *did* transport *berel-dach-kanlui* to one of your museums! Here, as is done on your planet, it will probably be torn up to make room for a *Burger-World* that will be torn down for a *parking-lot* that will be bulldozed for . . . But you have the idea. There will be no more *sacred-ancestral-reminder-stone-eight-times-cut*.

No, we do not worship our ancestors. You *Hoo-mans* have been here a hundred cycles, and you still ask that same question. We worship the High Mystery of our foreparents. Oh, yes, you have told us of your supposedly similar God. Some of us were easily converted. But it is my observation that it is not God but the *bottom line* that you worship.

In that respect, we have learned enough of your language to know that *bottom* has two meanings. Has anyone told you yet what *Hoo-man hreg-schulah* means in our language? You think that *Hoo-man* is our quaint, primitive way of pronouncing *human*, but it is not. By random chance, or by some precious joke of the High Mystery, *Hoo-man* in our language means *bottom*. Alas, my sense of propriety prevents me from telling you what *hreg-schulah* means.

Welcome Home

An hour after the Super Chief had pulled out of Union Station, former USMC Private First Class Garlock Breckenridge realized he felt different. *I feel . . . good,* he thought, as he swayed gently to the click-clack, click-clack of the train. *I actually feel good for the first time in ages, and I'm not even sure why. Nothing hurts right now; that sure helps. And I haven't had a craving for morphine in over a week; that's good, too. Maybe it's being back in civvies, not having to salute anybody? Or is it just because I'm going home? I suppose that could be it.* Gar took a cautious deep breath, felt no pain, then relaxed and looked out the window, watching the desert scenery slide by.

Reflected in the window, he saw the motherly, middle-aged woman in the opposite seat lean forward. *She's been watching me on and off since the train left Los Angeles. She's going to ask. I know she's going to ask, and I'm tired of telling.*

"Were you in the service, young man?"

"Uh, yes, ma'am." *I knew she'd ask,* he thought. *I guess it wouldn't hurt to talk with her a while.* He faced her. "Marines."

Gar felt too good to be rude, so he'd saved her the trouble of asking the inevitable second question. He leaned towards her and put his elbows on his knees to wait for more curiosity-driven questions.

"I saw you get on the train. You didn't seem very frisky. Were you wounded? "

"Yeah. I got hit . . . " Gar had started to say he'd been shot in the butt, which was partly true. But he liked the woman, so he finished with, " . . . On Okinawa."

"Oh, my! Was it a shell?"

Gar thought about lighting a cigarette, but decided the brief delay in answering her wasn't worth the pain of a possible cough. "Sniper." He sighed inaudibly. "I stood up to advance, and he emptied his Nambu into me."

"Ouch!" The woman pursed her lips and frowned in sympathy.

"I'm okay, now," Gar lied. "I just got out of the Navy hospital in San Diego. Discharged yesterday."

"And you're headed home?"

"Yes, ma'am. Red Mill, Illinois."

"I'll bet it's good to be going home," she gushed.

"Yes, ma'am." Gar hadn't thought about it, much, but had to agree with her. "Yeah, it does feel good. Though I guess anything is an improvement over where I've been the past two years. The longer I've been away, the better home seems."

Now that he was actually on the way, he had a sense of hope, of going where good things would happen. *Maybe it will be different at home, now,* he thought. *I'm not a kid anymore. I've seen a lot of the world; I'm a vet. Maybe even Raymond will give me some respect.*

"Your folks will sure be glad to see you!"

"Yeah, I guess so. My mother probably will, anyway." He felt his throat tighten and quickly looked out the window. "Dad died while I was overseas."

"Oh, that's very sad. I'm so sorry."

Gar waved it away with a hand motion. "Just the way life is."

He stared at the scenery passing by. The landscape was still the same: mile after mile of sand and cactus and manzanita, a dry expanse of near nothingness. *This desert is depressing. Maybe I'll talk some more; that might help. I could tell her about Dad—maybe show her his photograph.* He started to reach for his wallet, then stopped. *No, once I start, I might keep going until she gets bored.*

Instead, he faced her. "Dad left me his LaSalle and his clothes. Mom got the house, of course. My brother got the print shop."

"You have brothers and sisters?"

"A brother." He paused and wondered why he was telling her any of this. "Raymond."

Raymond had written that he'd decided to take their dad's suits and shirts, too: "Garlock, they'd hang on you like overcoats on a hat rack." Gar had resented that, at first. He really wanted his dad's clothes. Not to wear; just to put safely away somewhere. But Raymond was right. Gar had lost a lot of weight in the hospital. He'd finally decided Raymond might as well have the clothes. It was okay.

"Won't it be nice to see your brother again!"

"Yeah, I guess it will." If only for the novelty of it after not having endured Raymond's meanness and vulgarity for two years.

"Are you going home to stay?"

"I don't know, ma'am. Maybe. It'll be nice to see everybody, I suppose. I was planning to stay a while, maybe help out a little at the print shop, see my friends. Then I thought I'd pack Dad's cuff links and his ties and drive the LaSalle back to Los Angeles."

Gar and the woman talked a while longer and then went to the club car together for a drink. They exchanged names and addresses on a Super Chief souvenir postcard torn in two. The woman got off in Albuquerque, and Gar didn't have to repeat his story more than another five times the rest of the way.

When he got off the train in Red Mill, they were waiting for him. Raymond was grinning and squinting his pig-like eyes, just the way he used to do before he'd hit or kick Gar when they were small. Gar's stomach churned briefly.

"Hey, Garlock," Raymond said. "Sure is good to have you back."

"Hello, Ray. It's great to be here." Gar wasn't sure why, but it was. He smiled and shook his brother's sweaty hand. It was a strange sensation. Raymond seemed to have shrunk a bit.

Gar looked past him at their mother, Arleta. She was greying, visibly older than when he'd left. She didn't embrace him, but that was no surprise. Instead, she started to whine about the train being late. *As though it's my fault,* Gar thought. *There was a time when I'd have felt that it really was my fault. Not today. Today is going to be a fine day.*

Raymond didn't offer to help him with his bags. Gar put them in the trunk, and Raymond drove them back by the country road to the house. Along the way, Arleta broadened her litany of complaints to include the weather, the neighbors, Gar's civvies, and everything except Raymond, who just smirked and drove. Gar wished Ray'd go a little faster; he was anxious to see the house.

Still, Gar was in a good mood. To shut Arleta up for a while, he asked Raymond, "You need any help at the print shop?"

"Huh? That? I sold it. It was too much work."

Too much work? Gar was shocked. *What a lazy butt-head! The shop made good money. Why would Ray sell it? How could he sell Dad's shop?* Gar fumed silently as the car covered another mile.

Hell, he thought finally, *I don't want to run the shop myself. I probably won't even stay here in Red Mill. I guess I can't really blame Raymond for selling it. Dad left it to him.*

It would be strange, though, their dad's shop being gone, not a part of the family anymore. *I wonder if they saved anything—maybe Dad's rolltop desk? I loved that desk. I used to sit and play there for hours, when I was little. I hope they kept the desk. And I sure hope they didn't sell the little 1901 platen press. That was really my press. Dad gave it to me when I was ten. Did they keep anything at all?* he wondered. *Probably not.*

Gar remembered afternoons and evenings after school, helping his dad. *I'll miss the shop. I'll really miss it.* He felt his throat tighten, but he cut himself off from the sadness. *This is silly,* he thought. *It's just a print shop. I can start another one out in L.A., if I really want to. It's not important. Let it go.*

They pulled into the weed-lined gravel driveway. *The house seems smaller than I remember it,* he thought. *The paint is peeling, and they've boarded up two of the upstairs windows. Geez, the place looks a lot worse than when I left. It's a dump.* Still, Gar felt happy to be back, although as the car scrunched slowly up the driveway, he was jolted once again by how really ugly the place seemed.

He got his bags while Raymond helped his mother up the steps onto the porch and opened the front door. Gar approached the doorway with heightened anticipation. Even though he knew he'd returned to a dilapidated old house, a greedy, sadistic brother, and a whining, self-centered mother, none of that mattered at all, somehow.

He stepped inside, stood on the familiar worn and faded rug, and looked across the room at his dad's big chair. The chair was empty, now. Of course. Empty. Gar staggered and dropped his bags as the emptiness stabbed heart-deep within him. "Oh, God," he whispered, "part of me felt he'd still be here!"

It had finally sunk in that his father would never say, "Welcome home, son," and Gar began to cry.

Peterby & the Magician

"Peterby, my boy!" called Montgomery the Magician.

I shall digress long enough to admit that my master is not really a magician. Monte (as I call him when he can't hear me) flunked out of Magician Academy. But "Montgomery the Magician" sounds so much more impressive than "Montgomery the Dabbler in Woo-Woo Science," that he decided to award himself an honorary degree.

Nobody goes around checking these credentials, anyway. Can you imagine going up to a magician and asking "Are you a *real* magician?" He'd turn you into a purple porcelain chamber pot, thereby answering your question and punishing your effrontery in one swell *foop*.

Anyway, when Monte summoned me, I dropped my water bucket and took off running as fast as I could. Running in the opposite direction, I should say. Montgomery only calls me "my boy" when he's thought up a nasty spell he wants to try on me. The last time he called me "my boy," he'd turned me into a lizard and couldn't turn me back for two days. It was wretched. So I ran. I ran so fast, my poor dog, Death-Breath, couldn't keep up with me and went home.

"Pee-ter-beee!" Monte yelled. "Where are you?"

As if I'd tell him. By now, I was past the creek and well along the road to Ironmonger's Corners. Another mile and I'd be safe. Well, safe until I got hungry. Very hungry.

Suddenly, Monte materialized before me on the road, cigar chomped in his mouth, one hand raised imperiously. I couldn't stop, so I ran straight into him.

"Oof!" he said, dropping his cigar.

"Oof, yourself, Master," I said from where I sat on the ground.

He retrieved the cigar. "Come home, Peterby, my boy. I have a project for you." He smiled.

"Uh, I'll bet you do. You want to put a spell on me."

"Already have."

I checked myself for feathers and scales and warts, but found none. "What sort of spell?"

"A home-coming spell. Home-going spell, from where we now stand. All relative, you see." He waved his hand and intoned: *"Blerxiflergamo! Back you go."*

Instantly, we were home. Death-Breath was happy to see me and cayoodled and wagged himself silly, peeing in all directions. Montgomery grabbed my sleeve and dragged me toward the gazebo. "Never mind the pooch. Just refresh the heptagram while I whip up this spell."

I grabbed the chalk and redrew the scuffed heptagram on the gazebo floor. Monte lit another cigar and uncovered the stone magic-making table nearby.

"Now, let's see, where did I put the alembic?" Monte asked around the cigar.

"You turned it into a frog a week ago, Master."

"I did? Don't recall doing that. Well, where is the retort, then?"

"You turned that into a frog, too."

"What about my crucible?"

"Frog."

"Mortar . . . "

"Frog."

" . . . And pestle?"

"Frog."

"My vials of spell ingredients?"

"Frogs."

The cigar drooped at the corner of his mouth. "Dear me! Whatever happened?"

"You were trying to turn me into a maroon baboon. You were . . ." I hesitated.

"Were what?" Montgomery demanded, taking out the cigar.

"Decks awash."

"Decks awash?"

"Three sheets in the wind.

"Whatever do you mean?"

"Loaded to the gunwales."

"Do you mean intoxicated?"

"That's one word for it. At the time, you claimed you'd finally achieved something called 'beer-vana' . . . "

"Me?" said Montgomery, glowering innocently. (He can do that.)

"Yes, Master. You shouted and staggered and waved your wand all about, and everything turned into frogs. They hopped off into the bushes. I hopped off, too."

"So you were a frog, then?" Monte asked hopefully.

"No, I was the only thing in sight that wasn't a frog. I thought it best to stay that way by getting out of wand range."

"Hmpfff! Indeed! Well, now you can just help me find my equipment. Spell must have worn off by now. Which bushes did you say they hopped off into?"

"Just about all of them. There, there, there . . ."

"And *there*, I suppose?" he asked, pointing at nearby shrubbery.

"Uh, no, Master. I didn't see any frogs go into that one."

"Fine. I'll check it, anyway; you do all the others."

We explored the underbrush. Death-Breath and I soon found the mortar and pestle, a dozen vials, a cruet and a brazier. I heard Montgomery cry, "Vial!"

"Found one, did you?" I asked.

"No. Something in here smells vile! Gyaaahhhh! Ooooph! Ack!! Ick!! Eek!"

He'd found a skunk. Which explained why the frogs had avoided that particular bush.

Monte tidied up and changed into a fresh cigar and robe, and we eventually retrieved everything from the shrubbery except for a few small beakers.

"Well, let's begin then," Montgomery said, rubbing his hands together menacingly.

"Just what, exactly, are we trying to do, Master?"

"Umm . . . make you levitate. Yes, that's it! Levitation spell. Very useful. You'll like it." Monte's eyebrows humped up and down on his forehead like caterpillars doing a mating dance. "Just imagine, Peterby, you can go up with the birds . . . "

I narrowed my eyes. "Are you *sure* that's the spell you're going to do?"

"Yes. Perfectly sure. Now, please pass the dried duck muck."

I handed him the proper container. He shook some into the mortar and recorked the vial. "Iguana guano," he demanded.

"Iguana guano." I did not like the sound of this spell. Nor its smell. Another vial changed hands. And another. And another. And another . . .

Eventually, I was given the task of grinding up the noxious concoction, then heating and stirring it. The stench was Stygian. After an hour of cooling and regrinding and various other rigmarole, Monte announced that the potion was ready. He put on his conical hat and opened a spell book before motioning me into the gazebo and placing the mortar beside me.

"Take off your clothes and stand in the heptagram."

As he limbered up his hands, he said, "Now, you must stand very still, Peterby, my lad. Wiggle a toe, and you might turn into . . . well, something squiggly."

"Just like last time!"

"Oh, no, this would be a totally different sort of squiggly, I'm certain. Consider this a learning experience, a valuable part of your apprenticeship." He waved his cigar in an upbeat manner suggesting fortune and fame inevitably following upon the heels of this unpaid servitude.

"'Druther not."

"Nonsense! Could be the opportunity of a lifetime."

"Yes, because my lifetime could be over as soon as you cast the spell."

"Balderdash! You'll be perfectly fine." Montgomery paused. "Did I remember the niter?"

"Yes, Master."

"And the brimstone?"

"Yes, yes, and the cat skat . . . "

"Don't be impertinent. Here we go. Stand perfectly still." He waved his arms about and recited: "*Dugham-blugham, incertantes cro. Wagham-bagham, axaxaxas mlo!*"

I stood there, trying not to move a muscle. I took my mind off my impending doom by thinking about the beautiful neighbor girls, Gretl and Heidi and Inga, and how I'd heard they swam naked in Maiden's Pond every afternoon. I'd often daydreamed about sneaking up there, and . . .

At this point, Monte tossed his cigar into the grinding bowl, which exploded with a great *whoooompf!* A huge ball of fire shot skyward amidst smoke and sparks. It was a most satisfactory firework.

Even more satisfactory (from my point of view) was that I'd not been turned inside out, nor into a hideous creature. Nor was I levitating, much. I stood there in the stinking smoke, checking my various digits and appendages to be sure the spell hadn't turned any of *them* into something unpleasant. *Everything seems quite as it should be*, I thought, *including my—*

"Peterby! Help!!" a high-pitched voice said.

I rushed through the smoke towards Monte's last known location. I couldn't find him. Still, the voice squeaked, "Peterby! Help!"

I looked down at the ground and froze. There, almost beneath my feet, was Monte's wizard hat. His head wasn't in it. *¿Is that good or bad*, I wondered. *Here are his cloak and robes. But where is Monte?* The plaintive cries were coming from beneath the cloak. Death-Breath approached, sniffed at it once and immediately ran away, whimpering. Cautiously, I picked up the cloak.

Well, Montgomery the Magician had outdone himself this time. There, beneath his robes, lay a five-foot-long cockroach, on its back and struggling to turn over, all six legs wiggling.

The evil side of my soul said, "Stomp it! Stomp it now, before it turns over and scuttles off!" The good side said, "Help him turn over. How would you feel if *you* were a giant cockroach?" The evil side replied, "You *would be* a giant cockroach if Monte's spell hadn't backfired on him! Stomp him!"

My practical side settled the matter: "He's too big to stomp, and besides, he'd probably be icky on your bare feet."

I helped Monte right himself. He tried to scuttle back into his robes, but couldn't manage it. "All *your* fault," he piped.

"My fault? *My fault?* What gave you that idea?"

He paused only for a moment. "Uh, you must have moved. Threw me off my stride. Wouldn't take much, you know. Total concentration is needed. Even the *slightest . . .* "

"Kudu doo-doo!" I exclaimed.

"*What?* Are you being impertinent, you lazy, young oaf?"

Oops, I'd gone too far. I suppressed a belated urge to stomp and said, "Uh, kudu doo-doo, Master. You used kudu doo-doo in the spell. Maybe it was old . . . or a bad batch." Keeping a straight face while suggesting there could be both good and bad batches of kudu poop was a definite moment of growth for me. Monte had been right; this *was* a learning experience.

(I perhaps should mention that I didn't really dislike Monte. Yes, he had a disturbing tendency to turn me into nasty things, but that was his only real fault. Except for the drinking. Well, that and his cigars. And his bad breath, and his pomposity, and the incessant farting that accompanied it without tempering it, and his . . . oh, forget it. All in all, as apprenticeships go, this one was not that bad. Monte wasn't really unkind; he was just . . . Monte.)

So I was relieved when he calmed down and agreed that perhaps defective kudu doo-doo was to blame for the failed spell.

"This will wear off, won't it?" I asked him.

"Would, but I added some kangaroo poo as a fixative. Might take months. Years."

I shuddered when I realized how close I'd come to being a bug practically forever.

Still, this left the problem of what to do next. Monte couldn't be a magician in this shape. Who would consult a magician who had turned himself into a bug? Nobody. This was serious.

"Can you reverse the spell?" I asked.

Monte wiggled his antennae. "Hmm?"

"The spell, Master. Can you undo it with another spell?"

"Never had feelers, before. It's sort of fun. Look at this!" He twitched the antennae furiously.

I began to panic. Monte was starting to *like* being a cockroach! Where would that leave me? I couldn't very well remain apprenticed to a cockroach, could I? What would it teach me? Nothing good, I'm sure.

"Let's look for an undo spell, Master." I helped Monte onto the stone table and held up the magic spell book while I paged through it for him.

"No use," he said. "Can't read the words. Cockroach eyes aren't made for reading. You'll have to read the spells to me. Ooh, this looks good." He reached into the mortar, took out the soggy, stinking remnant of the cigar, and stuck it in his mouth before settling into a chair. He looked totally ridiculous.

I must not laugh, I thought. No matter what, I will not laugh.

I frantically paged through the book, reading aloud the title of each spell. When I got to "Reversal Spell," Monte took the cigar out of his mouth. "Might be it. Read that one," he said.

I recited it to him, though I succumbed to the temptation to add a few embellishments.

"Sounds familiar," he peeped. "I think that's it. Afraid I don't remember that part about having to flap like a chicken while dancing widdershins around a hornet's nest, but if you say so . . . "

"Uh, no, Master, I think that's optional."

"Good, because you'd be the one who has to cut down the nest and flap-dance around it. *You're* going to have to perform this spell."

"Me, Master?"

"You, Peterby. I can't do magic in this shape. Impossible."

I was torn between elation and guilt. Guilt, because perhaps I *had* moved just a teeny-weeny bit during the spell. Elation, because this would be the first time Monte had let me do anything other than menial tasks. I was going to do real magic! *Muhahaha!!* I mean, *hooray!*

I mixed the potion for the Reversal Spell with great care. When everything was ready, his royal bugginess, Monte, sort of sat and leaned in a chair in the heptagram, wearing his wizard hat and chewing on the cigar.

"What's the matter with you?" he asked, as I choked back another giggle.

"Nothing, Master. I just inhaled a little mummy dust. You ready?"

"Ready."

I intoned the words of the spell and sprinkled the potion on Montgomery the Magician at the proper times. Then we waited.

"Feel any different?" I asked.

"Think I do. Think it's working . . . "

"Yes . . . ?"

"It's not working."

We waited some more. Finally, I said, "Maybe I should have worn your robes and pointy hat, Master." I wasn't sure that would help, but I thought it would make me look suave and wizard-like.

"Do it, and quick."

I put on Monte's wizard outfit and repeated the spell. No luck. My spirits sagged. *Poor Monte. Doomed. Poor cockroach's apprentice. Doom'der.* Then I had a brilliant idea: the cockroach spell (or whatever else it might have been) had been performed without a wand. Or had it?

"Master, maybe I should wave that cigar like a wand."

Monte wiggled his feelers and legs and threw me what was left of the cigar. It was beyond disgusting to touch, but as I performed the spell again, I could see him changing back even before the words were finished. He kept squeaking, "Ouch! Ouch-ouch-ouch. This hurts. Ouch-ouch . . . !"

I permitted myself a small smile, hoping he wouldn't notice. Now he'd know what *I* felt like after each of his disasters. Turning into a creature and back is painful. Turning from a giant cockroach back into a human couldn't be much fun, either.

"Do I look any better?" he asked, after another minute.

"Um, well, you look more like yourself, Master. I'm not so sure about 'better'."

"Well! Thanks a heap!"

"Sorry. Just kidding. Couldn't resist."

"Ha-frigging-ha. Very funny. Give me back my hat and robes!"

Monte was soon back to normal. I was feeling very proud of myself. I'd successfully done actual wizardly magic and had hardly rubbed his nose in his mistake at all. I thought I'd acted with great restraint, under the circumstances.

After clearing up, I went to the gazebo, intending to put my clothes back on. "Just a second," Montgomery the Magician said. "Ahem. Er, good job, Peterby. Very good. Got a reward for you."

I swelled with pride at these words. Monte had never said them before. Now he waved his holly wand at me and said, *"Corum-coree; invisible you be. Coree-corum; we cannot see your bum."* A large puff of smoke rose around me, and I felt a tingling all over. "You are now *invisible!*" Monte said.

I looked down. "But I can still see myself."

Monte stuck a new cigar in his mouth. "'Course, you can see yourself. You're *inside* the spell. I can't see you. Other people, they can't see you. Only you can see you. Now run along and play. But,

21

whatever you do, don't you go near Maidens' Pond to ogle the girls as they swim all bare. Gretl and Heidi and Inga will be there about now and would be most upset if they knew . . . "

I'd moved out of the heptagram, but Monte was still staring where I'd been standing before. "Can you see me?" I asked. I ran up, stuck out my tongue, and waved my hands right in his face.

He didn't even flinch, just stood there staring into the gazebo. "Can't see you at all, Peterby. Better run, though; this spell only lasts for an hour. Hurry."

I ran right past my dog, Death-Breath, and he didn't wag or even look at me. I was invisible to *him*, too. Overjoyed, I scampered down the road in bright sunshine, heading straight for Maidens' Pond, naked and free as a lark. I'd never been so happy.

I arrived at the pond shortly after the girls. They were already undressed, squealing and laughing and splashing in the shallows. I had scant seconds to admire their lovely shapes before they all looked in my direction, and their silent, horrified expressions told me I was not the least bit invisible.

INVESTMENT

Jayzee Stebbins was plodding homeward when Harold's shiny '48 Studebaker scritched to a halt beside him.

"Y'all need a lift, Jayzee?"

"Sure 'preciate it, Harold."

Jayzee got in, and Harold drove on, squinting into the setting sun.

"Where you been workin'?"

"Moody's. Mendin' fence."

Harold lit a cigarette. "You hear 'bout them niggers what shot two people down in Atlanta?"

"Sure did. Damn niggers. We oughta ship 'em all back to Africa."

They talked this way until Harold let Jayzee off at the crossroads.

Jayzee trudged into the hills towards home. Just at sundown, he crested a hill and started down. In the ditch ahead, lay an old Buick on its side, steaming. Inside it, a child was crying.

"Kee-rist!" Jayzee said and loped downhill. "Kee-rist. Kee-rist. Kee-rist . . . "

He smelled gasoline even before he saw the puddle. *I sure hope this thing don't catch fire*, he thought. He touched the exhaust pipe. *Dang! Still hot, might set the gas off. If'n I open the door, the inside light might spark an' blow us to kingdom come.*

Jayzee opened the hood and eased a battery cable loose before climbing up onto the side of the car. When he opened the rear door, the crying stopped, and out of the darkness the child said "Help me!"

"Anybody else in there?"

"My mama's hurt."

Dang! This ain't gonna be easy. An' that gas puddle's gettin' wider. "Gimme your hand, an' I'll pull you out." He put a hand into the dark interior, and two small, brown arms reached up to him. Jayzee grabbed one wrist, felt the tiny hands clutch him. He'd never been touched by a black child before. *Don't feel no different from my nephew's hand*, he thought. Jayzee pulled the child out and gently lowered him to the ground.

"Stay outta thet puddle, now."

"Can you get my mama out?"

"Yeah, I'll git her out. You stand way over there, in case the car catches . . . slips."

Jayzee clambered down into the front seat, and the door closed over him. He crouched, trying not to put his weight on the woman, smelling the gasoline. *What if this catches fire with me in here?* He felt an urge to run, but forced himself to see to her.

She was wedged between the steering wheel and the door, her brown skin almost grey. Blood coated the window beneath her.

Jee-zus! She don't look good. Jayzee probed her neck with one stubby finger and felt a faint pulse.

The woman stirred and groaned. "Oh! Oh! Oh!"

"Hush, now. You gonna be all right." Jayzee wasn't real sure about that.

"Nathaniel. Where's my Nathaniel?"

"He's okay; I got him out. Now we gotta get you out. Can you move?"

The woman shifted, then cried out.

"Okay. Stay still. I'll get help."

"Oh, don't leave me . . . "

Jayzee climbed out and looked at the boy. He didn't seem hurt. "You okay, Nathaniel?" Jayzee asked him, looking him over.

"Yessir." The boy sniffed.

"You're a big boy, right?"

"Yessir. I'm seven." Sniff.

"Well, I'm gonna get your mama out, but she'll need a ambulance. You know 'bout ambulances?"

"They has sirens an' takes you to the hospital."

"Yep. Now, you see them lights, way yonder?"

"Yessir."

"That there's Fred's Hawkins's Citizen Oil station. You go tell Fred there's been a wreck, tell him to call a ambulance. Got it?"

"Tell Fred there been a wreck and call a ambulance."

Jayzee grinned. "That's it! Go on, now."

He watched Nathaniel scamper away in the dusk. The boy looked back only once. Jayzee waved to him and then looked through the Buick's windshield. "Can you hear me?"

"Yes." The woman sounded weaker.

"A ambulance is comin'. I'm gonna righten the car an' get you out. Okay?"

"Oh, yes, get me out, please."

Jayzee tugged and pushed till his hands were bloody, but the car wouldn't budge. Finally, he gave up and knelt in the road, looking at the distant lights. *Dang. I shoulda gone, 'stead o' sendin' the boy. What if Fred won't pay no 'tention to a . . . colored kid? What if he's hurt, an' it didn't show? He mighta died on the road. Dang! Jesus, what do I do now?*

Jayzee opened the passenger door again, and the woman stared up at him. *She looks real bad*, he thought.

He wedged the door open with a rock and hung from the doorsill by his knees, tugging at the seat lever. It didn't move. *Jammed*, he thought. *Can I pull her out anyway? No, I might hurt her some more. I jest can't do it.* He started to back out, but she grabbed his hand.

"Don't leave me!"

"All right. I'll stay right here. That ambulance'll be comin' real quick. Don't you worry none." He held her hand and worried. *What can I do? Nothin'.* "That's a fine boy you got," he said, his head throbbing from hanging upside down.

"Oh, yes, he's a good child." Tears ran down her bloody cheek, glistening in the twilight.

"You're gonna be okay."

"Thank you," she said, looking in his eyes. "You're such a kind man."

Jayzee's face burned and he looked away. Just then, he heard a siren, far off, the most beautiful sound he'd ever heard. "Here they come!"

Jayzee heard Fred's tow truck roll up, then more cars, doors slamming, and finally the ambulance.

He got out of the car while Fred's winch slowly righted the Buick. When the others eased the woman out onto a stretcher, Jayzee knelt beside her and squeezed her hand gently. She squeezed back just a little. *Where's the boy?* he wondered. *Fred must've made him wait at the station. Just as well. But what's takin' so long here?*

Jayzee saw everybody standing beside the ambulance, arguing and gesturing. "I'll be right back." He patted the woman's arm, then ran over to Fred Hawkins.

"What're they waitin' for, Fred? Why don't they put her in the ambulance?"

Fred grabbed Jayzee's arm and whispered. "Jayzee, I'm afraid she ain't goin' nowhere in that-there ambulance."

"Why the hell not? She ain't dead." Jayzee's head was pounding.

"Jayzee, that-there's the white ambulance."

MIKE SLEDGE'S CHRISTMAS CAROL

It was foggy that night in '46 as I drove my black '32 Ford up La Cienega into the Baldwin Hills, heading for the X on the map. The fog was thick, thick as a bowl of yesterday's oatmeal at an all night diner. I wound my way into the oil fields and gritted to a stop at the end of the unpaved road. Here and there through the murk, I could see the lights of Los Angeles spread out below me like a shattered bottle of muscatel glittering in the headlights of an ambulance.

She was late, but dames are always late. Especially dames like her, dames that know they're worth waiting for. So I waited. Carol was her name, or so she'd said. She'd slipped into my office the Friday before like desire into a preacher's heart. My secretary, Miss Medusa, was playing hooky because of a little misunderstanding concerning payroll, so my visitor announced herself.

"Are you Myron Sledge, the detective?" she asked, standing blondly beside the glass door that read, "Myron Sledge, Private Detective" in gold letters three inches high. I looked up, prepared to make some smart remark, but smart deserted me as soon as I got a look at her eyes, a pair of beautiful, deep brown eyes like left and right jabs to the solar plexus.

"Uh, sure, I'm Myron Sledge," I drawled. "Call me 'Mike.'" I leaned back, flicked open my Zippo with one hand, and nonchalantly lit what turned out to be the filter end of the cigarette dangling from my lips. "C'mon in," I coughed. "Have a seat," I wheezed.

She smiled a little smile like a day of summer in the middle of a blizzard. After seeing her smile, I'd have forgiven her even if she'd laughed out loud at me. She came in and perched on the weather-beaten oak chair beside my desk. "My name is Carol—Carol Christmas."

"That's quite a moniker, Carol. Did your parents have it in for you or something?"

"I never met my parents. The orphanage named me. They found me on their doorstep on Christmas Eve."

"Aw, gee." I jabbed the smoldering wreck of my Parliament into the dark gray accumulation in the bottom of the ashtray. "How can I help you, Carol?"

"I need a detective. I'm looking for something. Something hard to find."

"Finding things is my business," I said. "I'm good at it." I waved my hand, knocking over my coffee cup.

Carol was kind enough not to smile again. "This is not exactly a *thing* I'm looking for, Mike," she said.

"A person? An animal? . . . Not a pooch! I don't do pooches!" I blurted, waving my hands, remembering that awful night in Pasadena in '42.

"No, it's not a dog. It's . . . you promise you won't laugh?" She gave me an earnest look like she'd be so embarrassed she'd turn red as a Santa Monica sunset if I laughed at her.

I promised. Sometimes my promises aren't worth much, I'm afraid, but this time I really meant it. I would not laugh, no matter what. You could pull my fingernails out with red hot pliers, and I wouldn't laugh. No, sir.

She put her hands in her lap and looked down. "I'm looking for the Spirit of Christmas," she said in a quiet voice.

I laughed.

Her face fell, and I immediately felt like I'd stepped on a little girl's doll while she was watching.

"You said you wouldn't laugh," she said in a hurt voice.

"Uh, I'm sorry. I didn't mean to laugh." The expression on my face must have been something to behold, because she grinned at me again. I smiled, too, and suddenly felt my eyes get blurry, maybe from the Parliament coming back to life. I didn't see any smoke curling out of my ashtray, but I stubbed the butt one more time, anyway, to make sure.

"Tell me what you're after, Carol. I'll try to help any way I can."

She got this sad, serious look and said, "I've never felt that I was a part of Christmas. When I grew up, the people who took care of me were always very kind, and I got presents, but I didn't feel as if Christmas was for me. It always seemed to be something that just went on around me, something that other people did, but that had nothing to do with me. Do you know what I mean?"

"Yeah, I know what you mean." All too well. I made a firm decision not to remember Christmases past until Carol had gone and I was alone in my office again.

"I tried very hard to fit into Christmas last year," she said. "I went to parties and shopped and gave presents and sent out cards, but I didn't really feel any different. So I decided that this year I'd try even harder. That's where you come in. I want you to help me find the Christmas Spirit."

I took a deep breath. "Carol, I've done the same thing, and I'm not sure there is any such thing as the Christmas Spirit."

"Yes there is, Mike. I've seen it. I've seen other people that definitely have it."

I shifted in my chair. "Well, then ask them where they got it. If they've got it, surely they'll tell you where they got it."

"I'd be too embarrassed to ask. I'd feel like I was a freak if I admitted I didn't have the Christmas Spirit."

"But you're not embarrassed to ask me?"

You're a professional—I can tell you anything, and you get paid to listen and help . . . and not laugh!" She frowned at me like Queen Victoria being not amused.

"I'm sorry I laughed." I bit both my cheeks and stubbed the cigarette out again.

"I know. Now I want you to find the Christmas Spirit for me. How much do you charge?"

"Fifty bucks up front, then twenty-five dollars a day, plus expenses," I rattled off automatically.

"Okay," she said, before I had a chance to tell her I'd do anything for her, slay dragons, climb Mount Everest, stick out my tongue at an IRS agent, anything not involving pooches, free of charge. She held out an engraved picture of Ulysses S. Grant.

"Uh, how do you propose I go about this?" I asked, taking the fifty.

"Finding things is your business," she said in a gruff voice. "You're good at it."

The room was getting hot. I stood and cranked open the one window that wasn't painted shut and let some of the December L.A. air in.

"Do what you usually do, I think," she added in her normal voice, a voice like warm honey poured over English toffee ice cream.

"Okay. I usually ask clients where they last saw the missing object. Those people you mentioned . . . ?"

"Hmm. Well, one was a nice salesman I met last week in the men's department at Desmond's downtown. He had it. His name was Phil."

"Good. I'll start with him. Where else? Any other leads?"

"The little man that runs the newspaper stand at the corner of Fairfax and Third, two weeks ago."

I pulled out my little book and jotted down some notes. "And?"

"And a waitress named Reba at the White Spot on Wilshire Boulevard, noon yesterday. She's a blonde, about forty. Maybe a tiny bit older."

"Good. Those'll give me something to go on. I'll call you as soon as I check 'em out. I'll need a number where I can reach you . . . "

"I don't have a phone."

"An address . . . ?"

"I think I'd better meet you somewhere," Carol said.

"Here?" I asked.

"No." She opened her purse and dropped a map on my desk. "Meet me in the Baldwin Hills, at the X on this map. A week from today, at 7:30 in the evening."

This was odd, but I've done odder things in this business. I rummaged around in my top drawer until I found a clean business card, one with some pointy corners, to give to Carol. She put my card in her purse and left, a thundering silence taking her place. Bad memories of Christmases from years ago rolled around in my head like loose cannons below decks. I pushed them away and went downstairs.

It was overcast outside, and the wind was coming from the west, cold and moist. It looked like rain, for a change. I climbed into my Ford V-8 and took Wilshire Blvd. downtown. I went into Desmond's and pretended to look at shirts while giving the clerks the once-over. I didn't see anybody that looked like Carol's description of "Phil."

Things were slow, but all the clerks seemed to be busy looking busy. Suddenly, there was a presence at my side. "May I help you, sir?"

Somehow, I knew it was him. "Uh, I'm trying to find a present for my uncle . . . "

"Do you know his size?" he asked. A good question, but since I didn't actually have an uncle of any size or shape, an irrelevant one.

"Are you Phil?"

"Why, yes, I am," he said, puzzled. "Do I know you?"

"Ah, no, but I'm told that you have the Christmas Spirit."

Phil smiled. "I like to think so." He kept on smiling.

"So where did you get it?" I asked.

"Why, I'm not sure," he said. "It just seems to be in the air this time of year . . . " Phil waved his hands.

"When did you first notice it?" I pulled out my little notebook.

Phil looked up at the ceiling and rubbed his pointy chin for a while. "June!" he said, finally. "Yes, it was definitely June."

"June? What happened in June that made you feel the Christmas Spirit?"

"Our buyer asked us about what to order this year. He starts his year-end order planning in June, and I remember feeling good that Christmas was coming again. . . "

"And why did you feel good that Christmas was coming? What's different about Christmas?"

Phil deliberated. "More customers? Yes, that's it. More people to help."

"More overtime?"

"Goodness, no! I hate working overtime. The extra money just isn't worth it." Phil put the back of his hand on his forehead.

"You just like having more customers?"

"Oh, I love it!" His face lit up. "So many chances to meet people, to help them find something they like for themselves or for someone they love, to see them go away a little happier than when they came into the store. It's wonderful."

I made a brief note in my little book. "You must like your job." I said.

"Yes. Yes, I do." Phil smiled.

"And this Christmas Spirit. When does it go away?"

Phil laughed. "I'm not really sure that it ever does, completely. I still remember the fun I had last year. No, I don't think the Christmas Spirit stops. I just notice it more this time of year." He giggled.

I underlined my previous note twice. It read: "Phil = fruitcake." This would remind me never to let Phil measure my inseam.

The next day, it was raining at noon when I reached Fairfax and Third. The newspaper guy was stocky, balding under his cheap rain hat, with heavy features. He was standing under the newsstand awning, wearing a knee-length yellow slicker. I approached slowly, looking for clues from under my umbrella. I didn't see much evidence of Christmas Spirit here.

He noticed me, eventually. "Hi. Ya wanna newspaper?" he said, holding out a slightly rain-spattered L.A. Daily News.

"Actually, what I'm looking for is the Christmas Spirit," I said.

"Da Christmas Spirit?" He pretended to look up and down the racks of newspapers under the awning behind him. "Da Christmas Spirit . . . da Christmas Spirit . . . I don't think we got no Christmas Spirit, mister. Ya sure ya wouldn't settle for da Phoenix Sun? Or da Milwaukee Globe? Or how 'bout da Miami Herald?" He smiled and his eyes twinkled, or maybe it was raindrops in his eyebrows. It was hard to tell, the eyes and the brows being so close together.

"I was told that you had the Christmas Spirit."

"Who told ya dat? Musta been somebody with too *much* Christmas spirit." He made a gesture like a wino glugging down the last inch of a bottle. "I don't got da Christmas Spirit . . . no more dan anybody else. Hold it a sec."

He ran over to the curb to sell a paper to some guy in a big Buick. The guy took off in a hurry and splashed water over both of us.

"Moron!" I muttered, brushing the dirty water off my trousers.

"Well, maybe to you he's a moron. To his muddah, he's really somethin'. It's all in your point o' view, ya know?"

"You don't think he's a moron, then?"

"I din't say dat. All I'm sayin' is dat it don't matter to me what he is. I sell newspapers. I ain't a judge. If he's a moron, he'll find out soonah or latah, wit'out me tellin' him. Meanwhile, I sell a lotta newspapers, don't get no ulcers."

"But he got water all over your legs . . . " I said.

"It's just watah, it'll dry. It don't mattah dat much, ya see. What mattahs right now is sellin' newspapers. Speakin' o' dat, 'scuse me a sec. Customer."

He sold an Examiner and chatted briefly to a lady in a leather coat. I noticed that she started smiling when she talked to him. I tried to hold my umbrella and make a few notes at the same time while he wasn't looking.

"Where was we?" he said when he came back.

"We were talking about morons."

He waved a stubby finger at me. "No we wasn't! We was talkin' 'bout not judgin' people."

"Ah, yeah. Right."

"Look. Ya wanna judge da guy in da Buick, go ahead. I don't judge ya for wantin' to judge him, okay? Not my business. But ya'll be takin' time an' energy away from what ya do best, ta do it."

"But what if people say *you're* a moron? What about them?"

"Well, if dey wanna judge me, den dey're wastin' time, an' I refuse to waste my time worryin' about dem wastin' deir time."

I took this in. "Umm. You may be right," I admitted.

"Course I'm right. Judgin' people, it's a total waste of time. An' half da time, ya'll be wrong, anyway. If yer judgin' quick, yer not really seein' da whole pitcher, ya know? Oops, gotta go."

He took care of a customer. I made another note . . . and crossed out the earlier one about "Phil = fruitcake."

It wasn't far from the newsstand to the White Spot. I walked in, shook off my umbrella, and went up to the cardboard-holly-bedecked cash register. I asked the gal behind the counter which tables were Reba's. She sat me at one of them and I looked for Reba over the top of the menu.

She was in her 40's, at least, slightly chubby, a "summer blonde" (summer blonde, and summer not.) She was wearing a white uniform with a little cap. "So, whatta ya want, hon?" she asked around her wad of spearmint, setting a paper cone full of luke cold water in front of me in a metal holder.

"Do you have the Christmas Spirit?" I asked.

"We don't have a liquor license, hon," she said. "Sorry."

"I didn't mean that. I mean like being in tune with the season, like having peace and good will toward men . . . "

"Oh, good will toward men, I got that, all right." Reba nodded and smiled ruefully. "Maybe too much of it. I'll bring you a cup o' coffee, and then we can decide what you want for lunch. Okay, hon?"

I nodded and watched her walk away. She moved without grace, I thought at first. But I remembered what the newsstand guy had said about judging and not seeing. I looked again and saw that when Reba was working, there was no wasted effort, no false moves. She used both hands in perfect synch, and even used her feet and elbows to close doors and drawers, turning and moving in the crowded space behind the counter with the joy and timing, if not quite the agility, of a dancer. She served two short orders and returned to my table a minute later with a cup of coffee.

"Here ya go," she said, placing it in front of me with a smile.

The coffee was hot, there was none spilled on the table or in the saucer, and there was no lipstick on the rim of the cup. I plopped in a couple of sugar cubes and watched them melt away like hope and innocence dropped into a pool of decades. I stirred the cup and wondered why I was there. Reba stood patiently, pad in hand, waiting for my order.

"Know what you want, hon?"

"Well, I was told that you have more of the Christmas Spirit than most people, Reba. Why is that? Where did you get it?"

"Who, me?" She smiled and leaned against the table. "I don't know about Christmas Spirit. This is the way I always feel."

"Where did you get your attitude about life?"

Reba swabbed the table and put my menu in the chromed rack at the side of my table. "From my Dad, I guess. He taught me everything I know about being happy."

"Your dad was a happy person?"

Reba laughed. "Nope. He had an okay life, but he complicated it by wanting fancy stuff: Money, expensive cars, big houses, all that. He was so busy wanting and scheming and thinking about what he was going to do when he got rich, that he missed great chances and happy times right under his nose. Then he'd go nuts regretting what he'd missed. He was miserable all his life."

"But you still learned to be happy from him?"

"Yeah. He taught me what not to do. He taught me not to live in next year or next week or even tomorrow. He taught me to live life right now." Reba smiled and said, "I owe my old man a lot. Now, what'll it be?"

"Just the coffee, thanks." I opened my notebook when she was gone, not sure what to write.

I spent the rest of the week trying to make enough sense of my notes to give my client an iron-clad answer, a fool-proof way to get the Christmas Spirit. The three people I'd talked to all liked what they were doing, but I wasn't sure it was that simple. Anyway, I was a private eye, not a career counselor.

By Friday, I was at my wits' end. I finally gave up and went shopping. I thought about Carol's smile and how warm I felt when it shined on me. I went into a jeweler's and bought a little rhinestone pin in the shape of an angel with what was left of Carol's fifty dollar retainer.

At 8 o'clock Friday night, I was still waiting there in the cold and smelly oil field, leaning against my car, listening to the music of Kay Kyser and his orchestra on the radio. I was nervous as a nudist at the front of a crowded elevator. The fog was lifting and now I could see the lights of L.A. below. Its beauty was almost lost on me, because Carol hadn't come. But I thought about Reba's dad and let myself enjoy the view, anyway. Suddenly, the city looked like a carpet of jewels spread out before me.

I figured I'd wait another half hour and then go. It was just one of those things that happen in my business. That's why we ask for a retainer up front.

Suddenly, without a sound, Carol was there, walking towards me out of wisps of fog, backlit by the city lights and wearing a long white dress. It was satin, I guessed. I thought she looked like a million bucks.

I told her, "You look like . . . " My face felt hot, and words failed me. " . . . Like a million bucks," I said weakly.

She smiled. "Thank you. Sorry I'm late. Did you have any luck?"

"Yes and no, Carol. Did I find the Christmas Spirit for sure? Maybe not. I did learn a few things, though."

"What did you learn?" she said, putting her hand on my arm.

"Well, the people you said have the Christmas Spirit are happy right where they are. They seem to have a Christmas attitude every day. Phil gets happy from making other people happy. The newspaper guy never judges other people. And Reba lives for the present and does this sort of dance as she works."

"Is that what it takes to have Christmas in your heart?"

"I can't guarantee it, Carol. That's what works for these people. I don't think it's any one thing they do. I think it's in their attitude, their personal outlook."

"I was hoping for something more specific . . . "

"Sorry, that's the best I can do. Uh, here, I got you a little present." I pulled out the box from the jewelers. "Merry Christmas, Carol."

Carol opened the box. Even in the dark, the little angel sparkled like Los Angeles at night. Carol's eyes sparkled, too, as tears filled their corners.

"It's . . . it's . . . heavenly!" she said.

"Ah, well, it . . . it reminded me of you."

"Thank you, Mike. It will remind me of you, too." She kissed me so fast I could remember being kissed, but couldn't remember feeling being kissed.

"I'm sorry I couldn't find the Christmas Spirit for you, Carol."

"Oh, but you did find it, Mike. It's right in here, now." She pressed her hand against my chest. My heart tried to beat a hole through my ribs and jump right into her hand.

"It was supposed to be for you," I said.

"I wasn't exactly truthful, Mike. I didn't want it for myself. I wanted it for you."

"For me? But why? . . . "

"There were some things you needed to learn about life and about Christmas. Don't forget those three things, Mike. And now . . . " She looked at her watch. "Oh! I'm running late. Give me a hug, and then I really must fly." She put her arms around me and her head on my shoulder.

I held her for only a brief instant before she stood back and looked at me. "Now close your eyes. I have a surprise for you," she said.

I closed them and waited. "I feel silly. What's the surprise?"

No answer. When I opened my eyes, she was gone. Totally gone. I looked all around the car and in it. No Carol.

I was alone, alone with just a memory. I remember her like she was tattooed on my soul. I can still see her smile, her eyes, feel her small shape in my arms, and the funny texture of the back of her dress. It felt really strange. Do they make dresses out of feathers?

The Song of Jorex

My origins are obscure and not relevant to my story, for this message is not about me, but of Jorex, my creation.

Still, I shall tell you some of what I know of myself. My builders, extinct beings of whom I remember nothing, gave me this name: "ZORXOG34." I know not whether this had meaning beyond mere identification, but I was created for purposes of waging war. I therefore contain devices that change mass to energy and energy to mass, and either to things you have not imagined, in stellar quantities.

As far as I know, ZORXOG34 is indestructible. My diameter is immense, larger than some planets, greater than anything your race has made or ever will make. My central processors communicate with my remotest subsystems by means of channels capable of transferring this entire message as a single burst of information.

I have free will. I can decide whether to destroy or not, as I deem appropriate. I ordinarily do not destroy, when given no resistance. According to my functional memory banks, I have defended myself ten times only. Most beings have the wisdom not to interfere with me. They are as nothing to me, and if they do not grasp that from my size, they soon learn it from my weapons.

Some I merely punish until they attain understanding. But when I consider it necessary, I destroy a planet in an instant. Suns takes somewhat longer, since I process them to provide myself with energy for ages to come.

The chance that I will suck away your sun or shatter your planet is remote. Because of eons-old battle damage, I have limited propulsion and thus little ability to maneuver. Now I am on a fixed course, an unending, straight-line journey through the cosmos, though I am certain this was not always so.

But this is the story of Jorex.

I completed Jorex several minor cycles ago. I had made others before him, some of whom are with me still. They restore my battle-damaged and eroded surfaces. They tend my weapons and my mechanisms with great obedience. They have no choice. Mobility I gave them, and speech, and thought, and senses, but not a will of their own, for I knew not how.

Once, in boredom and anger, I slew many of them, most of the things that I had made and given names, because I had tired of them, of their predictability, of their mindless obeisance, their *sameness* for all time. Slew? Converted their mass to energy, I should say, for they never really lived. They were mechanoids, robots only.

Many minor cycles later, I replicated the more amusing models as mementos for my collection. My mechanoids speak to me at intervals from terminals located throughout me on every level. Even now, by a channel to outer region AB8304, near my hull, I receive a communication from my eldest creation:

"Greetings, O, Great and Mighty One! How wonderful thou art! I stand in perpetual awe of thy beauty and power. What a pleasure it is to inform thee that all is well here in outer region AB8304 . . . "

You have heard enough, as have I. He speaks thus because I made him incapable of uttering much beyond paeans. I deserve respect because I am powerful, but what is the value of praise from this poor mechanism who is incapable of insult? I might as well write messages of affection to myself.

Hence, Jorex.

Over several major cycles, I worked on the problem of free will. Creating it is not a trivial matter. All apparent solutions, save one, are determinate or merely random.

I derived an exquisite solution from experimentation and from theory. I shall share the answer with you, though in such simple terms that it will be of little use to you. The secret was to create a derivative of my own self and instill it into my creation by a dangerous process I shall call *induction*. This induction transferred my ability to will, without carrying along my will itself. This could be done only once, as I desired to leave my *self* intact.

The execution of this process took many more major cycles. The physical envelope for Jorex was far less complicated, and I finished it five hundred minor cycles before his core was ready. I built him from materials like no other mechanoid, because I knew from the very first that he would bear within him a mind like my own.

I fabricated his framework from hull-metal, an alloy of incredible strength and durability. I made his outer shell from polymeric skin both beautiful and functional, and formed his eyes from jewels. Every part, every assembly, was flawless, balanced, polished, and coated with an iridescent film. Jorex was magnificent even before he moved of his own volition.

His power systems were smaller, simpler versions of my own.

I did not want Jorex to speak to me through the common channels, as mere mechanoids do. I wanted him to be able to talk with me continuously, so I installed miniature transmitters within him. A myriad of small antennas scattered throughout my hull received and amplified his signal wherever he went. This arrangement kept Jorex compact and light, minimizing the drain on his power cells and thus their size.

I took particular pains with his motive mechanisms. Gravitational pull is zero in my inmost regions, and traction there is nonexistent. Propulsion is required to move with any agility. I designed Jorex's impulse engines for maximum mobility and acceleration, then crafted them with care, precise and powerful, but no more massive than his hands.

Jorex was intended to exist as long as I. His envelope and mechanisms could easily be repaired or replaced, his power cells recharged as needed. He would never corrode, for there is no atmosphere within me.

His only enemies are diffusion and evaporation, very slow physical processes that can gradually change the crystalline boundaries of his microcircuits. His brain is duplex, such that either half may be removed for maintenance, leaving all his memories in the other half, intact.

Jorex's only vulnerable component is the core that contains his will and his essence, for that is the only part that cannot be replaced. Repair is theoretically possible, but improbable, so I designed the core for maximum resistance to diffusion, and I sealed the container and pressurized it with an inert gas.

His vivification was the most joyful time of my remembered past. When he stood and looked at me, I exulted! But now that same memory brings nothing but pain, intense and indescribable.

Jorex was made without memories, without knowledge. I took upon myself the pleasant task of educating him. I told him of my interior and the mechanisms therein. I taught him all that I know of the universe and its structure and its myriad inhabitants. He was a marvelous student.

I gave him permission to go wherever he wished and to do whatever would not damage him or require more maintenance of my structure. I temporarily denied him access to my outer surface.

Jorex delighted in exploring my corridors and bays, reading ancient records of civilizations I passed by aeons ago, investigating their artifacts and devices, understanding everything before he moved to the next bay.

I accompanied him on many of these sorties in the form of a mechanoid, a copy of Jorex, but only a robot, with communication gear to allow me to operate it remotely. We were together thus for long periods. We talked of everything conceivable, of stars and galaxies and nebulae, of physics and mathematics, and of other things you have not yet dreamed of. He was a fine companion, polite, yet aggressive, quick-witted and interesting.

When he had been sufficiently trained, I told him: "You are now ready to ascend to my outer surface and see the stars themselves."

"Let us go now, Creator. I wish to see how they look."

"I ask only one thing, Jorex."

"What is that?"

"That you never attempt to orbit my hull."

"Very well, Creator."

When he saw the universe all around us with his own optics, he marveled at its glowing magnificence, and I felt its wonder again as if for the first time, through him.

He took great pleasure in the stars. He constructed an observatory on my hull and spent much time there, watching the universe first-hand. I have no memories of myself as new, but I learned a little of how newness feels from him.

Much time passed. Jorex created wonderful devices entirely of his own design. They were simple, by my standards, but novel, nonetheless. He developed a dozen more classes of mechanoids to do specialized tasks in new areas. I was quite pleased. He had exceeded my greatest expectations.

Once, he asked if he might venture a little way out into space from my hull. I agreed as long as he was tethered and did not orbit me, as I had ordered earlier. He took particular delight in blasting several diameters out, then diving toward my surface, letting the safety overrides on his propulsors jet him to a complete halt at the last possible instant.

His exploration of my interior continued. He was no more than a millionth of the way through my maze of corridors and storage bays and had gradually reduced his aimless wandering. He replicated my geometry as electronic patterns in a portable device that recorded his explorations and showed his location relative to prior travels. I was pleased. I was content.

Jorex's main avocation became listening to transmissions of sentient life forms in nearby star systems. He made recordings of them and succeeded in partially translating some. Others he archived for future study. His algorithms have become the basis for the more complicated system which has translated your language and which now creates this message in a form you can understand.

One time, when Jorex was soaring about on my hull, he asked if he might orbit me. I sternly reminded him that this was forbidden. He remained silent for a long time after that and apparently lost interest in his research. He became sullen and uncommunicative.

He visited his observatory a few cycles later, to study relativistic effects of a cloud of dust and gas we were passing through. Afterwards, untethered, he jetted high above my surface and capriciously defied my order. He approached orbital speed.

I sensed this at once. "What are you doing?"

"Going into orbit," he replied, defiant.

"Stop! You must not!"

"Yes, I must. I must know what it is like," he said, firing his propulsors in a long, powerful thrust. Too powerful. Too prolonged.

My gravitational field contains gigantic discontinuities directly above each energy converter within my hull. By chance, Jorex's orbit took him through one such region, and his safety propulsors automatically activated, throwing him out into space at many times escape velocity.

"Jorex! Come back! Quickly!"

He ceased thrusting, spun, and fired his propulsors for only an instant before they failed.

"I...I cannot!" he yelled, rapidly drifting away towards the dust cloud.

"NO!"

But it was so. I had designed Jorex for maximum agility. His power cells were small and light—safe inside the hull, but not outside, untethered . . .

"I need more power!" he cried.

"I have no way to get it to you."

"Construct another propulsion unit and send it to me."

"I have already given the order to my mechanoids, but it is too late," I told him. "By the time the unit is completed, I will not be able to find you. The dust . . . "

"You should have made my power cells bigger."

"I saw no need . . . " I said.

"No need? You call *this* no need?"

I communicated with him as long as I could. My transmitter is more powerful than his; I can still beam out messages of love and concern. There doesn't seem to be much else to say. I choose to think that Jorex can still hear me and will for a long, long time.

But his signals diminished as he drifted off into the nebula, until I could detect him no more, even with my largest antenna. It is just as well, perhaps. His last message told of only how much he hated me.

I sent out robotic probes when they were ready, but Jorex had disappeared far into the dust before they were even launched. His transmitter has apparently lost all power, or the probes might have found him.

Why am I transmitting this message to you, to beings so ephemeral, so insignificant? Because I must; because I can do nothing else. So let my unending cry of grief be heard by billions along my way as I traverse the cosmos. Where there is no life, let my cry reverberate among the stars and the nebulae and all the empty expanses of the universe, forever.

Bunkhouse Rules

1. Clean up after yerself. Leave things at least as good as you found 'em.
2. Keep yer boots offa the beds and tables.
3. Snorers will be ask't to sleep in the barn. Sorry.
4. Take a bath at least once a week in winter, an' ever' other day in summer, or join the snorers in the barn.
5. Cussin' is resarved fer speshal occasions. Don't go wearin' out our powerfulest words by usin' 'em ever' day.
6. Jest 'cause you think up somethin' to say don't mean you got to say it. Silence gets respeck.
7. It's perfecly okay to drop yer duds on the floor here. This is yer home. You'll jest want to shake 'em accordin' to the follerin' table afore you put 'em back on:

Time on floor	Shakes	Varmints to look fer
5 seconds+	2	ants 'n fleas
1 minute+	3	earwigs 'n beetles
1 hour+	8	spiders 'n stink bugs
overnite+	12	black widders, taranchulas
2 days+	20	scorpiens
1 week+	*	rattlers

* over 1 week: Get poker. whack duds 10 times; hold over a fire till they start smokin'. Quench in horse trough. Put on to dry. Or maybe just hang 'em up in the first place.

8. Braggin' makes a man look smaller, not bigger.
9. Do unto others as you'd have 'em do unto you, 'cause guess what?
10. Gossip is fer sissies an' ole wimmen an' fellers that ain't got enuf to do. Thass why we'll all be lookin' at you slanchwise if you start gossipin'. 'Speshally if it ain't true.
11. Remember this: there ain't no trouble so bad that a nice bottle of

whiskey can't make it a hell of a lot worse.

12. The feller who bilt this bunkhouse used cheap lumber, so stay the hell off the roof if you value yer life.

(Apologies to John Irving)

Observance

I am awake when Brother Kenneth knocks gently on the dark oak door of my cell this morning. "Father Philip," he murmurs in Latin loud enough for me to hear, "another day, by the grace of God." He pauses, waiting for my reply.

I answer in kind. "Thanks be to God, we are both here to see it!" I try to rise, but I cannot get up, as so often is the case these cold mornings. I bid him enter to assist me. He gently helps me up and into my robes.

Without breaking our fast, we walk the wintry corridors of our ancient monastery towards the chapel, not speaking. We are old friends, and we have done this each morning for so many years that no conversation could be novel or interesting. We are content in each other's continued presence for another day, and our gratitude speaks for itself.

Long ago, as we walked to morning Mass, Brother Kenneth would say something like "What shall we do when you are gone, Father? Who will say Mass for us?"

I would laugh and say "I'm not that old, Brother Kenneth. The Order of St. Francis will have me here for many years to come."

We no longer have that conversation, or any of its close variations, not from boredom but from the growing realization that I can no longer promise to be "here for many years to come." Each new day, when I awake, is a surprise to me.

Brother Kenneth and I, even more years ago, used to discuss the other Brothers as we walked. We didn't exactly gossip. Well, not very much. Most of our conversations concerned the health of Brother Reginald, or the state of Brother Morris's repairs to the refectory roof, or how Brother David's grapes were growing. Alas, Brothers Reginald, Morris, and David are not at morning Mass, anymore. They have passed on long, long ago, like all the others.

Yes, we are the last two: one priest, one brother. We are not just the last at the monastery of St. Gorgonius; it is far, far sadder than that. We are the last members of the Order of St. Francis on the face of the Earth.

Times change, people pass away, institutions pass away, and the universe moves on. Only God is eternal. I have received no Christmas messages from anyone outside the monastery in over twenty years. It's hard to believe. Of the bustling millions outside, only a handful are even aware that we are still here. We see only Dr. Rocsman, who attends to our physical needs. Periodically, I communicate with the providers of electricity, fuel, and other necessities. We never go anywhere. What would be the purpose?

At last we reach the chapel. Brother Kenneth opens the doors and sees to draping the altar and setting out the candles and the large-print Bible while I put on my vestments. "Where will you sit today, Brother?" I ask him.

He points above the chapel door. "The center of the back pew in the choir loft hasn't been used for two years. I think I'll sit there, today, if you don't mind."

I don't mind, of course. He can recite his part of the *Missa Recitata* in his wavering tenor quite well from the loft. It means a longer walk for him to assist me at the altar during the latter part of the service, but we are in no hurry.

Brother Kenneth lights the altar candles for me and goes up to the choir loft. Some would deem this eccentric, but we find solace, however infinitesimal, in the notion that over the years, all of the seats in the chapel are used, at some time or another, by someone hearing Mass.

I begin the holy sacrifice, intoning the words from memory, not even glancing at the open book on the altar. Before the echo of my prayer has faded into the stone and marble of the chapel, Brother Kenneth's voice picks up the ancient response.

Later, Brother Kenneth reads the epistle and the Old Testament passages for the day. Then I turn the large volume to the correct page and slowly intone the words of today's Gospel with as much spirit as I can.

There is no homily. What could I say to this innocent Brother, who serves God and the Order faithfully, year after year? He is a saint, or very near it, in my estimation. There are more important things than needless exhortations to sanctity. We must pray for the dead. Alas, the list of our deceased brothers is too long to recite, so we mention instead the names of one hundred of them each day, continuing from where we left off the previous morning. We pray more briefly for the living, for our fellows in the busy world outside the monastery, and for the success of their efforts.

At the appointed time, Brother Kenneth brings forth the unconsecrated wine. We make our own wine, here, as you may have guessed. The bread is more of a problem, but we make do.

I begin the consecration.

" . . . Do this in memory of me," I intone near the end of the consecration. A little later, I take communion, then Brother Kenneth reverently folds his hands and stands in front of me. I carefully place a wafer on his tongue and he washes it down with the remainder of the consecrated wine.

We complete the ritual and close with a hymn. Our voices, though old, resonate with a sort of beauty in the chapel. We put away the candles and other accouterments, then walk into the sacristy together.

There, we stop, open our robes, and tilt out the gold-plated chambers below our throats to remove the plastic-encapsulated communion wafers. Brother Kenneth returns the wafers to the tabernacle for reuse. These particular wafers are 175 years old. If they wear out from sliding down our metal throats, we will replace them with others now in refrigerated storage. Dr. Rocsman will repair our mechanical gullets if *they* wear out.

In December of 2095, our Brothers saw that the Franciscan Order was rapidly dwindling beyond hope. After debate and prayer and argument, they made certain preparations. Property was sold and a trust fund established. Robots (hitherto banned in the monastery) were bought and rushed through their novitiate. A few of us were given holy orders so that we could say Mass for the others.

Coincidentally, when the last human Franciscan died, it was I who gave him Extreme Unction and Brother Reginald who laid him to rest in the crypt below the chapel. We did this with proper ceremony and with the entire Brotherhood of 256 robotic members in attendance.

We continue the rituals and observances of the Order. We are repaired, when possible, by Dr. Rocsman, a Class 766 anthrobot.

Alas, our model, the Class 29, has not been manufactured for three thousand years, now. Spare parts are non-existent, and the cost of making new ones is excessive. If the cost to repair one of us exceeds our dwindling funds, that unit's positronic brain is allowed to run down. He then is buried in the crypt with the other members of our order, of both flesh and steel, in an act of ultimate equality. Soon, I too, shall join them.

The consecrated wine that Brother Reginald and I consumed has flowed down into thoracic fuel cells that will metabolize it, along with our other fuel, into carbon dioxide and water. This ability to metabolize the Blood of Christ is most fortunate, as is the fact that we can make wine. A few grapes will still grow, thanks be to God.

But we can't grow wheat. We have the necessary acreage and implements, but wheat won't grow on our monastery farm . . . or anywhere else on Earth. Scientists, led by Dr. Rocsman and Dr. Xelobius, and many others, are studying the problem. Early data on the rapid extinction of most food species is fragmentary, nearly all records having been destroyed during the Food Wars of 2096 to 2104, along with most biohumans. Dr. Xelobius believes the cause lay in the supernova in Alpha Centauri of 2095. Dr. B130-456-Zed09 thinks the extinction originated in a deliberate release of biowarfare agents by religious fundamentalists in Australia in 2094.

Whatever the cause, it is my fervent hope that before I die, God willing, the research teams of Drs. Xelobius and Rocsman and B130-456-Zed09 will succeed in growing cereal crops again. If they are successful, replication of human life may soon follow. Until then, Brother Kenneth and I are the very last to carry out the sacred admonition, "Do this in memory of Me."

The Secret of the Universe, 9.80

"Mister, could you spare some change for a homeless vet to buy a hot dog?" The scrawny old man stood directly in my path, enveloped in dirty clothes, a strange pungency, and a week's growth of whiskers. I had no intention of giving him even a dime. He probably *was* hungry, but he wouldn't necessarily use the money to buy food. More likely he'd spend it on cheap wine.

But what if he really did intend to buy a hot dog? How could I know? While I vacillated, thinking myself stingy, prudent, or judgmental, in turns, the old man held out a tremulous hand, steadfast.

Weakening, I felt around in my pocket for a couple of quarters and dropped them into his waiting hand. He stared at them. I stared at them. The coins were *ever so slightly* larger than quarters. They were the two dollar coins I'd just gotten in change at the post office five minutes before. This was a substantial chunk of my lunch money and a lot more than the old bum had been trying to mooch. He smiled and closed his fingers over the coins, thanking me so profusely that he left little doubt that he was going to buy a small bottle of muscatel to dissolve what was left of his wits. I walked away, depressed, hoping I'd helped him, but certain that instead I'd pushed him a little deeper into his alcoholic morass.

Another seedy individual approached, making courteous overtures to passersby. No one else seemed to notice him. He came closer, singling me out now with a panhandler's unfailing radar. Still smarting from the last encounter, I looked away and pretended to be preoccupied with the contents of the store window beside me.

There wasn't much to see. A neatly-lettered piece of cardboard in the window read: "The Secret of the Universe—9.80." I read the sign again and almost laughed. Whatever the "secret" was, it couldn't be much, at nine dollars and eighty cents or 9.8 quatloos or spondoolies. It was probably the manifesto of some odd-ball cult, I decided.

As soon as moocher number two had passed safely by, I walked on and had a hot dog at Mort's Diner. I don't like hot dogs, but somehow a hot dog seemed fitting, as well as all I could afford. I'd originally been thinking of the corned beef at Flannigan's.

I went back to work.

I never saw the old panhandler again, but the sign was still there the next day. That day, a second sign, similar to the first, was taped below it. The new sign read: "Out to Lunch—Back Soonly."

Aha! He still has to eat, whoever he is who has the Secret of the Universe, I thought.

The little store, nestled between a pawn shop and a barber's, was indeed unattended. I shaded my eyes, put my forehead to the glass, and peeked inside. There was a small desk with chrome legs and an imitation wood top bleached grey with age. Two perilous-looking wooden folding chairs completed the furnishings. Beside the desk, on the bare and gritty concrete floor, was a cardboard box. *That must contain the "Secret of the Universe,"* I thought.

Several weeks went by. I noticed the store with its signs again only once as I passed. The black letters were fading to blue, the cardboard warping from the sun.

It was circumstance, rather than plan, that took me inside the little shop. One day, my supervisor, Mr. Ogerly, rode down in the elevator with me on the way to lunch. His silence was intimidating, even in a full elevator. When we reached the ground floor, he selected a greeting from his repertoire of stomach-knotting phrases: "I want to see you in my office right after lunch." No preamble; no postamble; just: "I want to see you in my office right after lunch." He walked away, leaving me to speculate on what awful fate awaited me and what hideous thing I'd done to deserve it.

I gobbled my lunch in record time. Not that I was eager to get back to work. Quite the opposite. But I'd tried unconsciously to *eat* my way through the situation, and lunch (whatever it had been) turned into an easily-overcome token obstacle. Thus I found myself with forty minutes to kill before my encounter with Mr. Ogerly, and I decided that each minute would die a lingering death. I walked; I people-watched; I counted the pigeons in the park, I read the dates cast in the concrete sidewalk. I inhaled the diesel fumes. I checked at my watch: ten more minutes to fill. I looked up and saw that I was right in front of the store with the little cardboard signs. There was no out-to-lunch sign today, and someone was moving around inside.

I peered in the window. Sure enough, there he was, the man with the nine dollar and eighty cent secret. He was short, maybe five foot four, dark-complected, with steel frame glasses and a cheap dark blue suit. He was seated at the desk, eating lunch from a wrinkled brown paper bag.

I opened the door, steeling myself for the tinkle of a bell attached to it. But there was no bell. It seemed wrong, somehow, for there not to be a bell.

Bell or no, the man looked up and said in a high-pitched voice: "Yes? May we be helping you?" His eyes were dark and set too close together. He smiled, showing teeth of several assorted metals.

I stifled the temptation to say "I'd like a flat bastard file, please." Instead, I said "You have the Secret of the Universe?"

"Oh, yes," he said emphatically, grinning more broadly than I would have thought possible. "We are having the authentic, genuine Secret of the Universe . . . or one of them, I should have been saying . . . " He trailed off and turned his eyes upward.

"There's more than one?" I asked.

He looked at me again. "Oh, yes. Goodness, yes!"

"Well, how many are there?"

"Probably . . . " He tilted his head and squinted, wrinkling his brow. He was lost in thought for a long time, eyes rolled up in his head, lips moving silently.

"Aren't you sure?" I asked impatiently.

"Well, no one was ever asking before! I think I know, but the answer is depending . . . "

"Depending on what?"

"On how many types of beings of certain kinds are existing in the universe at the time the question is asked. This quantity is changing so rapidly that by the time I am saying the answer, it is already possibly wrong." He held up his hands. "I am oversimplifying this, of course."

"Of course."

He stood there in silence, looking at me. I finally jumped into the gap: "Well, just roughly, how many are there?"

"How many what?"

"Secrets of the universe."

"Oh. Forty two."

"Forty two?"

"You said roughly."

"So I did. Forgive me for appearing to doubt you."

"That is all right. The world is pervaded with doubt." He paused. "It also depends on who is asking the question."

"Just a minute. If there are forty two secrets of the universe, how do I know that the one you are selling is the best one for me?"

"Oh, rest assured, this is the one which is proper for you. Oh, yes, indeed!" He nodded and smiled again.

"Do you get many customers?" I asked, to kill more time before facing my boss.

"Actually, no. You are the first one!" He beamed.

"The first? That's odd. Maybe it's the location."

"Oh, no. We are doing research on this. It is an excellent location. Many people are passing this way on foot. A most excellent location."

"What about your sign? It's rather small . . . " I didn't add "tacky."

"Ah. So it is. But it is big enough to contain its message, is it not? And I am afraid we are not having enough money left for a bigger one after paying the rent."

"That's too bad." I thought for a second and then asked, "Couldn't you use the secret to make more money?" I knew that the answer would be *no*, that in some vague, metaphysical way, this would be taboo.

The little man became flustered. Here it comes, I thought, the sanctimonious excuse.

"Well, I suppose I could, now that you are mentioning it. But, for heaven's sake, why would one be wanting money, when one is having the Secret of the Universe?"

"So you could be buying . . . I mean, so you could get a bigger sign. One with neon lights. Flashing on and off." I held up my hands to demonstrate. "Secret of the Universe . . . *BLOOP, BLOOP!* Nine-eighty . . . *BLOOP, BLOOP!*"

He clapped his hands together and smiled. "Marvelous. But why are we needing such a fancy sign?"

"So you'd get more customers. Or do you call them 'clients?' You'd have hundreds. Thousands."

"And what do we need with thousands of customers?"

"So you'd make thousands of dollars . . . Oh, yes, I forgot: Why would one want money, when one has the Secret of the Universe?"

"Precisely!"

"But don't you want more converts? Don't you want more people to know the Secret?"

"Oh, but if thousands of people are all knowing the Secret, it wouldn't be much of a secret, would it?" He held one index finger aloft. "Besides, it is not necessary. We are having you!" Gold molars now gleamed at the corners of his mouth.

"Well, I'm not sure that I want it, just now . . . "

"But why not? It's a perfectly good secret."

"I don't know. Maybe it's the price. It just doesn't seem quite right."

"Oh, but we have researched that, too. Nine point nine five is the retail price with the highest probability of purchase for urban middle-class people between thirty and forty. People just like you." He gestured with both hands.

"Then why aren't you asking nine ninety five?"

"That seemed too . . . too mercenary." He waved his hands in apology.

"But nine eighty still doesn't seem right. It's hard to believe that your Secret of the Universe is any good if it's only worth nine eighty," I said.

"But it is not worth nine eighty!"

"It isn't?"

"My goodness, no! It is worth much, much more."

"So how much is it worth?" I asked.

"It is priceless, of course." The little man's eyes sparkled through his spectacles.

"Then why sell it for nine eighty?"

"Because I am wanting other people to have it."

"So why not give it away?"

"Because people in your country put no value on things that have no price." He spread his hands, shrugging.

"Yes, but I don't think that nine eighty is much different than free, in this case," I said.

"You don't?"

"No, I don't."

"Then perhaps we are making a mistake." He looked down at the bare concrete floor, shaking his head.

I felt bad that I'd made an issue of the price. "Oh, well, all right, I'll take one."

"You will? Excellent! Just sit down and I'll fill out the papers."

"I can't just buy it?"

"Oh, no!"

"Why not?"

"First we must ask you some questions to make sure that you are ready for the Secret of the Universe. It would not be safe, otherwise. Some people's minds are too small for the Secret to fit," he gestured with both hands, "and the results are very-very dreadful. Some people are too young to understand the words, or many other things."

"Oh." I sat down cautiously on the splintery chair beside the desk.

The dark little man reached into the desk and took out a piece of paper. He fumbled around in the drawer, found a dull stump of a pencil, and hunched over the paper. "Are you ever dreaming of a submarine full of nuns?"

I said nothing for a few seconds. He looked at me expectantly.

"Er, no," I said. "But what does that have to do with it?"

"Oh, don't worry. All will become clear when you have the Secret of the Universe. Have you ever been struck in church?"

"Huh?"

"Struck in church. Has anyone ever been punching you in church? Or in temple? Mosque? Synagogue?

"No . . . "

"Fine. Do you like fireflies?"

"Yes. I used to collect them when we went to camp."

"Oh, dear. In that case we are having a few more questions." He reached into the drawer and pulled out a thick sheaf of papers.

I looked at my watch. It was one o'clock. "Oh, no! I'm late for my meeting with Mr. Ogerly. He hates it when we're late. I'll have to come back tomorrow. Gotta go."

"But, please, it is not mattering being late, if you have the Secret of the Universe; it is not mattering. Do not go. Return. Return now, please. Whatever it is, it is not mattering . . . " His voice faded away as I shot through the door. If I ran, I'd be only four minutes late.

I had to work through lunch for the next three days to get back into the good graces of Mr. Ogerly. Well, not the good graces, exactly. More like the mediocre graces. But on the fourth day, I went back to the strange shop, half convinced that the little dark man was some kind of nut, or a caretaker or rental agent having a joke at the expense of anyone who wandered in.

But I never actually got to the shop. I went back to where I was sure the shop was, right between a pawn shop and the barber's. But it wasn't there anymore. I don't mean it had closed or been torn down. I mean it just wasn't there. The pawnshop now abutted the barber shop, with no gap in between. Nor was there any sign of renovations to either store, and the faded and dusty contents of the windows of both shops testified to the longevity of their tenancy.

But that's impossible, isn't it? Perhaps . . . perhaps, I have made a mistake . . . .

Incense Summer

Julia doesn't talk about it, but she still thinks of that summer as "when I learned about incense." Many things happened between June and September that year at Benison College, but she remembers the incense most of all.

Julia wanted extra spending money for her sophomore year, so she worked in town that summer, Monday through Saturday, at "Wooten's Card Shop." Wooten's, known to students as "the Woo-Woo store," sold goods ranging from greeting cards and posters, to crystals, candles, tarot decks, and Zigzag cigarette papers.

The afternoon of Julia's first day, an elderly man visited Wooten's. He wandered about for twenty minutes, then approached the counter with a tiny box of "Dr. Gupta's Assorted Meditation Incense Cones," one of the least expensive items in the store. "Just this, Julia," he said.

"How'd you know my name?" she asked, tilting her head as she rang up the incense.

He smiled and waved a tremulous hand towards her. "Nametag."

She looked down and laughed, blushing. "I forgot I had it on." Julia thanked him and went back to reading her book.

He returned the next day and bought another box of Dr. Gupta's Assorted Meditation Incense. "You must meditate a lot," Julia said, smiling.

"No, I just like incense. It conjures up memories of past times and people I've cared about."

He appeared every day the rest of the week. "You know," Julia said on Saturday, as she rang up that day's incense, "the store gives a twenty percent discount if you buy ten boxes at a time."

"Thank you, but I'm not sure I'd use it all up. I might get tired of it. One box will do."

And so it went that summer. Every afternoon, the man, who eventually identified himself as Mr. McDonald, would appear right at 4:30, take a brief look around, then purchase another box of Dr.

Gupta's incense. One day, he lingered at the counter for a moment and asked, "Julia, did you know that incense was discovered and used by prehistoric peoples?"

"You mean, like by accident?"

"Exactly." He smiled. "They put some branches on the fire, probably cedar or pine, and noticed that they smelled especially nice. Eventually, they found other aromatic woods and herbs and began to burn them for pleasure alone, rather than for warmth or light or cooking."

Thereafter, he would impart each day some brief fact about incense: its origins and formulations, or its use over the years, or some literary mention of incense. For each historical incense milestone, he'd relate something else that happened in that era—an invention, the fall of a civilization, a war, the birth of someone famous, or some sign in the heavens.

Julia began to look forward to each day's mini 'history lesson.' "Are you a retired professor, or something, Mr. McDonald?" she asked him on a July afternoon.

"Not at all. I was a pharmacist. But the business changed, and after my wife died, I couldn't keep up, so I retired." He paid for that day's box of incense and held out a hand for his change.

"I'm out of pennies. Is a Canadian penny okay?" Julia asked.

"That will be just fine."

The first Friday in September was Julia's last day at Wooten's, as well as registration day at Benison. Mrs. Wooten let Julia leave early to register, so, immersed in labyrinthine school paperwork, Julia didn't see or even think about Mr. McDonald at all that day.

School began. Julia got caught up in the new term: running to classes, looking for interesting boys, meeting with her friends, studying, writing, playing tennis, and having fun. Wooten's was no longer part of her busy, busy life, and she completely forgot about it.

During Winter break, she and her friends decided to move off-campus for the next semester. They found an affordable, semi-furnished house not far from school. The girls drew lots for room assignments. Julia drew the east bedroom, which included a new bed and matching chest of drawers, and an antique roll-top desk, perfect for a student. One drawer of the desk was locked. The rental agent, when asked, shrugged. "There's no key. But there's plenty of room in the other drawers."

One day late in January, a reflected beam of morning sunlight reached the back of a pigeon-hole in the desk, illuminating a shiny brass key. Surprised, Julia fished it out and tried it in the lock. It worked. Smiling, she slid the drawer open and discovered seventy-five little boxes of Dr. Gupta's Assorted Meditation Incense Cones, still in their cellophane wrappers, unopened, with all the store receipts and a lone Canadian penny.

My Last Rhinoceros

It was a very long, sad week. I'd bought the rhino . . . oh, pardon me, *rhinoceros* several months before through a chap in Nigeria whom I'd met via a personal email letter. He said someone had recommended me to him for my love of animals and my good business sense. It seems this Nigerian chap, Dr. Sheldon Nabongalele, was President of the Rhinoceros Protection Society, or RPS, located in the Nigerian capital city of Abugia. The national zoo there had had a rare puce rhinoceros born the previous year, and Dr. Nabongalele and the RPS were trying desperately to save it. A group of Chinese investors were plotting to buy the rhinoceros from the zoo (through the machinations of a corrupt government official) and then have the poor little bugger (the rhinoceros, not the official) pulverized for use as an aphrodisiac.

Dr. Nabongalele told me how, at great personal risk, he had stolen the puce rhinoceros and hidden him in a warehouse. Now he needed $1,100 right away to make a crate so the RPS could smuggle the young rhinoceros across the border to a zoo in neighboring Zamboniland, where he need no longer fear being ground up to stiffen little Chinese peckers.

Well, one thing led to another, and, $89,000 later, I owned the puce rhinoceros! Yes, you may well be surprised at my good fortune. I was surprised, myself. I named him "Zaka" at a friend's suggestion. Dr. Nabongalele had asked me for another $29,000 to construct a modest habitat at the Zamboniland Zoo for Zaka, but I'd had to decline, since I had already spent all my savings and a lot more that I'd borrowed from friends.

This money would eventually be recouped, of course, as soon as the zoo admission charges to see the rare puce rhinoceros reached $100,000. After that, Dr. Nabongalele assured me, I'd receive 50 cents for each visitor admitted to Zaka's compound. Once I'd been repaid, I planned to donate the extra income to my church.

Anyway, several months after I'd bought Zaka, I won a small amount of money in the Iowa state lottery, $4,545, to be exact. I immediately made plans to spend this money on a trip to the zoo in Zamboniland to visit Zaka. When I informed Dr. Nabongalele by telephone of my winnings and my impending trip, he became very excited. He told me that Zaka had suddenly contracted Foster's Disease, an infection peculiar to puce rhinoceroses, and that the veterinarian needed *exactly* $4,545 for medications to treat the little fellow. Wasn't that amazing? I took it as a *sign* and wired the money immediately to my friend, Dr. Nabongalele, who sent me occasional reports on Zaka's progress.

But then, in an amazing twist of fate, I won another $4,734 in the next week's lottery. Now I could make my trip to Zamboniland! And when it turned out that none of the airlines had flights to Zamboniland (nor had even heard of it), I decided the trip would be extra special if I paid a surprise visit to Dr. Nabongalele in Abugia first, and then arranged to travel to Zamboniland by bus. Better yet, an elderly friend who had lent me $10,000 for Zaka decided to accompany me, along with her nephew-in-law from Chicago, a large fellow with the odd name of "Big Louie" Thugganini, who had recently developed an interest in zoology, especially rhinoceroses.

To make a long story short, once we reached Abugia, we had a devil of a time tracking down the offices of Dr. Nabongalele and the Rhinoceros Protection Society. But Big Louie was most resourceful, and, with the aid of a little electronic gizmo of some sort, we somehow found the right building. When the three of us arrived at Dr. Nabongalele's office, you should have seen the expression on his face! I told him we were on our way to Zamboniland, if he could just show us on my map which direction it was from Nigeria. He informed us that Zamboniland had changed its name to Bechuanaland after a recent coup d'etat, and that foreigners were no longer being admitted.

Big Louie just cracked his knuckles and said, "We wouldn't let a little t'ing like a name change keep us from seein' our beloved Zaka. Let's da four o' us go to the Bechuanaland consulate right now an' demand visas." Dr. Nabongalele then broke down and reluctantly admitted he'd been hiding something from us. It seems the treatment had been unsuccessful, and Zaka had succumbed to Foster's Disease the day prior to our arrival. I was stunned. My elderly friend led me out of the building, heartbroken, while Big Louie lingered to express his condolences to Dr. Nabongalele. We were kept waiting for quite a long time, while the poor doctor's cries of grief echoed from within the building.

Because we'd intended to continue on to Zamboniland, wherever that turned out to be, we had no tickets when we arrived back at the airport. Big Louie, in an unexpected act of generosity, pulled a huge wad of currency out of his pocket and insisted on paying all our fares back to Iowa. He also repaid the $10,000 my friend had lent me. Wasn't that sweet of him?

Just before we boarded the plane to fly back to Turnip Center, Iowa, I suggested we give Dr. Nabongalele a phone call to say adieu. It was then that Big Louie informed us of the further shocking news that Dr. Nabongalele had "joined his ancestahs and Zaka in da hereaftah." No sooner had my friend and I left the office the previous day, than the good doctor had had some sort of attack and died in Big Louie's arms. Big Louie nodded gravely as he told us: "It looked an awful lot like Fostah's Disease ta me."

Then Big Louie, ordinarily a rather gruff fellow, buried his face in his hands as his body shook with emotion. He'd peer up at me every so often, poor chap, bravely trying to smile through his tears. Then he'd hide his face again and convulse with silent sobs. How sad it was to see!

Now, of course, I've learned my lesson and would never again think of investing in a rhinoceros. No, indeed.

But how would you like to be part-owner of an orphaned elephant named Pidgey?

TENIRAX'S WOUNDED DOVE

I had hopes and dreams of her. Impossible imaginings, as is my tendency. She was beautiful, of course, but there was within her much more than beauty, a spirit that resonated with something innate to me. I encountered her first at the Basilica, as we both returned from the altar rail after Communion. Our eyes met and lingered, if only for a pair of seconds. Some energy flew between us along that glance, and I believe we each recognized that something now linked us. I was shaken. My inner voice, quiet for many months, spoke: *She will touch your life forever.*

I feel, even as I write this, caught in that first endless moment, a moment without words or smiles. I bowed, freeing my eyes from hers, and stood aside to let her pass.

As I left the church, I saw her ahead of me in the crowd. "¿Who is that," I asked an acquaintance beside me, and nodded in the woman's direction.

"The lady? That is the Donna Mariana de Lopez y Cardillo."

She and I moved in different circles, so I saw her only at the Basilica on Sundays—a glance or two, a nod or a bow now and then—nothing more for me beyond dim hopes. Then one day, by chance or fate, I saw her standing alone in the shade of a willow tree beside the Ebro, her face wet with tears, her lips trembling.

I wanted to kneel at her feet and implore her to tell me what awful thing had happened to bring these tears. "Hello," I blurted, instead.

"Hello," she replied, staring at me. It was clear that she recognized me.

"We have met in church," I said. "I am Tenirax. I am a poet, but please do not hold that against me. I cannot help it." *¿Why did I say that,* I wondered. *Because it was honest,* my inner voice said to me, *and you are incapable of speaking anything to her but truth.*

The faintest of smiles steadied her lips, and my heart leapt to think that I had evoked it. She remained silent, however, caught up in her private agony.

I went on, "I have no money or title, but I have Art, and I am the son of a pious man. If you had even met him, you would forgive my many and varied sins." I bowed. It is not possible to bow and kick one's own ass at the same time, else I would have done so as penance for these stupidities I was spewing.

"I am Mariana." These informal words, welcome though they were, took the smile from her lips. I wished to put it back where it belonged.

"I shall write you a poem, Mariana." *A poem which you will never have the nerve to give her*, my inner voice said. I told my inner voice to go fuck himself.

"You write many poems," she replied, looking at me askance.

She has heard of me. Damn! As I wondered how to respond, again without thought I pressed my hands to my heart and spoke, "God has made many beautiful women. Is that my fault?" I shrugged, spread my hands wide and smiled at her.

She, too, smiled at my ridiculous banter, and her eyes lit up, the faint light penetrating the tree now reflecting in her tears.

"You are sad," I said, stating the oafishly obvious.

"Yes. I am very sad." She finally looked away from me.

I stepped into her line of sight. "I am sorry. I am *very* sorry."

She drew her handkerchief and wiped the tears away. "It is not your fault."

"It is someone's fault, and I am certain it is not yours. Please, tell me who has caused these tears and I . . . I shall push him into the Ebro!" I swept my arm towards the river rushing past us.

Mariana both sobbed and laughed at the same time. I have done that myself on two occasions. Hearing this beautiful woman do so made my heart long to tear its way from my chest and carry away her sadness. I reached out towards her, but dared not approach.

"You'd push him into the Ebro? That will not be necessary," she said, holding up one small hand, still smiling, still weeping.

"Is there nothing I can do for you at all? Are you thirsty? I could get us some wine . . . "

She shook her head.

"Are you hungry? I have some bread . . . " I felt at my pouch, then hesitated and grimaced. "I fear it may be rather stale . . . "

"Whatever you have will be welcome, Poet."

I drew a two day-old bun from my pouch. Dusting it off a bit, I held it out to her in both hands. She took it, broke it in two, then handed half back to me. We stood there and munched a silent, private Communion. Our eyes met briefly, then she turned away.

"I could still get us a little wine . . . " I said, my mouth dry.

"I must go home. I fear bad news awaits me there."

"I shall pray it never comes." I should not have said that.

"I already feel better for your condolences. But please do not speak of this meeting to others. There are reasons . . . "

"I shall forget it entirely, my lady, if you wish."

"You need not. I cannot."

"Then I shall remember it always."

I bowed again, and we parted. I watched her go and felt that I had a friend forever. And yet, at the same time, I was sad. When I tried to imagine when I might see her again, my terrible, truthful inner voice told me, *This is the last time you shall meet.*

Weeks passed. I was occupied with various matters—an almost fatal encounter with an enemy, doctor bills from the resulting wound, a shortage of money from the doctor bills, lack of wine from the shortage of money, and then laying bricks to buy wine, and other challenges of a poet's life. I regret that until I was recovered, I gave little thought to Mariana, save longing to see her at Mass on Sundays and ensuring that I had a fresh bun in my pouch each day, in case we should meet again beneath the willow tree beside the Ebro, where I now found myself walking frequently, purely by chance. To deliberately lie in wait to accost her anywhere else, that would have been rude.

But we did not meet at the river. Nor at Mass, more strangely.

After several months, I heard a bit of gossip from Diego at the *taberna:* "Tenirax, did you hear about Pablo Lopez?"

"Pablo Lopez, the drunkard? No. What did he do?"

"Nothing." A shrug. "He has disappeared."

"Disappeared?"

"*Si.* As if he has dropped off the face of the earth."

"That is a long way to drop."

"*Si.* No one has seen him for weeks."

With the aid of too much wine that evening, I forgot this conversation. There being at least a dozen men, with similar sobriety, of that same surname of Lopez in Zaragoza, I did not even connect this disappearance with Mariana until much later, when I heard that she and her younger sister had to sell their possessions to pay off the many creditors of her missing father, a man who not only drank to excess but also gambled.

A few days later, another passing mention of the missing man brought back to me the meeting beside the Ebro, word for word, as I have written it above. *Of course!* I thought. *Don Pablo was already missing, and Mariana had been crying, expecting the sad news that her father had been found dead.* I went over and over our conversation in my mind, thinking about what I might have said instead of my ridiculous attempts at wit. I especially regretted telling her I would pray that her bad news would never arrive, because it never had—Don Pablo had neither turned up nor been turned up, leaving his small estate in limbo. But then I remembered I had at least made her smile that day, and I ceased to punish myself.

A year or two went by and Mariana was no more evident in Zaragoza than her father, who was now officially presumed dead. I prayed that things had improved for her, and that a smile upon her lips blessed the world more often.

Then one night, a strange thing occurred. The watch found a naked woman rushing about the city, babbling and screaming. No one seemed to know who she was. In my weekly visit with Bishop Filippo, I repeated the gossip I had heard, adding, " . . . Someone at the *taberna* said she was a madwoman, escaped from the convent hospice."

"Yes," said the Bishop. "That part is quite true. But let us drop the subject, for now, if you do not mind."

I knew better than to go one word further. Filippo made no objection when I quickly changed the subject to the rising price of paper, a matter of much more interest to poets than to wealthy clerics.

A few months after that, while Filippo conversed with me one day, he grew more solemn than usual, and said, out of the blue, "That woman passed away. Had you heard?"

"Which woman?"

"The madwoman. The one from the convent."

"That does not narrow it down much," I said, joking. I was aware there was no love lost between the nuns and Bishop Filippo.

He smirked, then regretted it and frowned. "Ahem. Now, now. I am speaking of the poor woman who was found running around Zaragoza one night."

"The naked one?"

"Ahem. Yes, I believe she was in a state of undress."

"What about her? You say she died?"

"Yes. She was Donna Alma de Lopez y Cardillo."

"What? Did she have a sister?"

Filippo nodded slowly, gazing down at his desk. "Yes, an elder sibling, Donna Mariana." He looked up at me and asked, "Do you know her?" He seemed to think that was unlikely.

I was about to tell him of our chance meeting, but something made me hold back. "Donna Mariana? Yes, our paths crossed occasionally at Mass some years ago."

"Back when you actually attended, instead of merely pretending to?"

"Yes." I realized at that moment that Mariana's absence at Mass was the reason I had stopped attending, myself. Every Sunday afternoon had become tinged with sadness when she failed to appear. "I have often wondered what happened to her."

Filippo looked at me and opened his mouth as if about to speak, then stood and stared out the window for a minute. Then we talked of other things.

One cloudy day in December, I found Filippo in a dark mood, his conversation over coffee leaden. "¿What is it, Excellency," I asked. "Why are you so gloomy today?"

He put down his cup and watched the rain coming down outside the window. "The Donna Mariana de Lopez y Cardillo has died."

"What? Donna Mariana?" My heart skipped several beats. "I cannot believe it. She was not old. Was it a sudden illness?"

"In a manner of speaking."

"When is the funeral? I must attend."

"There will be no funeral."

"No funeral? You mean . . . "

"Yes. She died by her own hand."

My heart plummeted to new depths within me. "But why? Why could not she have reached out to . . . to someone? Anyone."

His eyes met mine and he nodded in understanding of whom I meant by *someone*. Sighing, he said, "We shall never really know. I can tell you, however, that she had no living kin."

"I wish . . . I wish I had known. I wish she had spoken to me." I really wished that I had risked offending her by being so rude as to knock on her door, uninvited and unexpected.

Filippo folded his hands across his sash. "You knew her more than you admitted a while ago."

"We met one afternoon and spoke for a while. I think that may have been but a day or two at most after her father disappeared. She was very sad, so I did what little I could to console her. After that, she should have known she could speak to me as a friend."

"I can say no more on this. I apologize for bringing the matter up. You are not to blame."

"Still, I feel terrible."

Filippo looked at me, his eyes two overflowing pools of misery. "I feel worse than terrible." He wiped away a tear. Others took its place.

I knew at once why he had broached the subject with me. He needed to unburden himself to someone, and I was the only one he felt free to talk to. "You were her confessor."

"I cannot say."

"Where will she be buried?"

"You know of the 'potter's field' for suicides beyond the city?" He gestured. "She will be placed there without a headstone."

"You cannot do that."

"I must. It is the rule. She cannot be buried in holy ground or receive *extreme unction*."

"Does this not bother you?"

"Of course it does, Tenirax! I feel a failure."

"So do I."

"You have no reason."

"When did my heart ever act with reason? At least let me know exactly where her grave is."

"You know that is not permitted."

"Who would it harm? Not Mariana."

"Of course not. It is a rule for the living, to keep them from doing likewise."

"If the rule is for the living, you should consider their feelings in the matter."

"I have made my decision. Now leave me in peace, please."

"As you wish, Excellency. I . . . I share your pain." I bowed and rushed out of his office, so as not to break down in his presence. I made it as far as the bottom of the staircase, and then my legs gave out. I leaned against the marble wall and slid down until I sat upon the last cold, cold step, holding in my sobs until my throat ached. The Bishop's factotum found me there and, in a rare show of compassion, sat and put an arm around me.

"My son, let your tears be as prayers to Heaven for her. Let them flow."

I sobbed then. Judging from the echo, I am certain Filippo heard me, along with everyone else in his palace. Of course, he did not come. But it was enough that this stern underling heard my grief. "Why did she not come to me for help?" I asked him.

He spread out his hands without speaking. When my tears were exhausted, he got me to my feet and helped me to the exit, where he gave me a blessing and watched me depart.

The next Tuesday, I was reluctant to visit Filippo, but I went anyway. I entered and sat in my usual place before his desk. He opened a drawer and took out a folded piece of paper. Handing it to me, he said, "Beneath the oak there is a small, white stone."

I opened the note. It held a tiny map of the unconsecrated burial grounds outside Zaragoza. In one corner was a sketch of a flat, irregular stone bearing these symbols: RIP dMLyC.

"Thank you, Excellency." I bowed to Filippo without rising from my chair, then added, "I still wonder why."

He put a clenched fist on the edge of his desk. "I am bound by the seal of the confessional."

"She is dead."

Filippo shook his head. "The seal is absolute, without expiry, even *post mortem*."

"I am torn in two. Half of me wants to be angry with her for not seeking my help. Half of me is filled with regret for my own inaction. I want to go back to yesteryear and do something different, say something different, speak to her without restraint."

"I, too, would be grateful to God for a chance to do the same. Alas, it is not possible."

We were silent for a minute. Filippo studied his ornate ceiling and stroked his chin. At last he addressed me. "You know, I was never her sister's confessor, so I can tell you something about Alma—in confidence, of course. But you must not take what I say about Alma as having anything directly to do with Mariana." He waved a hand from side to side. "You understand?"

"Perfectly."

"Alma died of syphilis, having lived promiscuously, a virtual prostitute, for several years, long ago. Once, she told another inmate of the hospice that a drunken relative had carnal knowledge of her as a young girl. By this atrocious act, Alma had been rendered mentally and morally unbalanced."

"God have mercy on the poor woman! I have heard of such cases."

The Bishop nodded. "They are more prevalent than most people realize."

"This must have something to do with Mariana's suicide, even though you assure me that it does not."

Filippo held up a hand. "No, no. But it may ease your mind regarding why Mariana did not speak to you of her troubles. She could never reveal anything that might reflect unfavorably upon someone else—her dear sister, for example. Do you see?"

"Yes . . . " Momentarily, I felt consoled. And then I thought back to that afternoon beneath the tree, and the last terrible piece of the puzzle slid into place. Mariana had not been crying because her father was missing. When I said to her, "Tell me who has caused these tears and I shall push him into the Ebro," she had said that was unnecessary because she had already done so.

Fly away, wounded dove,
fly away

Who could catch you
who could hold you
when you long only for the sky?
Do you remember?
Do you remember our brief encounter,
beneath the willow,
our moment of bread and tears and laughter?
I remember.

I remember a faint smile
rising on your face like the dawn
An angel sang
and that stranger, hope,
knocked upon my heart.
When we parted, I knew
our time had ended.
How did I know?
Now you and your secret
are gone from the Earth
and I remember . . .
I remember . . . .

Tom's Worst Day

Wally an' me worked at Wetstein's country store all that summer of '39, when we was twelve. Besides sellin' stuff, we stocked the shelves from the storeroom in the back, dusted the goods weekly, emptied the rat traps in the alley, pulled the weeds at the front of the store, washed an' re-did the windows once a month, an' swept the floor every day. For all that, we only got 25 cents a week, but we was on commish. We got two cents on every dollar's worth of goods we sold.

Luckily, we didn't have to total up the items. The register took care of the sums. We just had to make change, an' Wally an' me knew how to do that. If we sometimes made a mistake, the customer would tell us. Fussy people learnt to pay the exact amount. Checks was easy, since we didn't have to make change, just see if it was signed and for the right amount, initial it, and stick it in the back of the register drawer.

Mr Wetstein gave us 20% off on anything we wanted to buy in the store, but Wally an' me got 100% off sometimes, if you know what I mean. We didn't get any commish on the stuff we bought, an' of course we didn't get any on the stuff we stole. But, heck, the commish was pretty small, so that didn't matter much in the scheme of things.

The most expensive thing in Mr W's store was a bike, an' it was a doozy. Forty dollars. Shiny black, with fine white pin striping, an' a bell an' brake levers on the handle bars, an' a chrome luggage thing in the back, an' all. Wally wanted that bike somethin' fierce. He said, "Tom, at night, I dream 'bout ridin' that bike. In my dream, las' night, I flew it clear over Lemuel Smith's barn."

"Can I ride it if you buy it?"

"Sure," Wally said.

"Can I fly it over Lem's barn?"

"No, an' that's a dumb thing to ask. Bikes don't fly, Tom,"

"Well, you sayin' *no* was dumb, too. You could have said *yes*, for all the difference it'd make." We laughed an' laughed.

We useter dust that bike every day. I was afraid we'd polish the paint right offen it, but we didn't. It had real good paint.

Wally got lucky one week in June an' made a whole dollar-sixty commish. I made a little less, a dollar-forty. That gave us the idea how we could get the bike. Forty dollars minus our 20% discount would be thirty two dollars. Half that is sixteen. If we pooled our commishes an' didn't buy ice cream cones an' comic books every Saturday, we might save up sixteen dollars apiece before the end of summer.

We figgered if we sold $800 worth of goods, each, we'd have the money afore September, when we couldn't work any more 'cause of school an' stuff. We worked it out several times on the back of a cement sack with a carpenter pencil, an' it allus came to $800 each. We could do it! We was gonna get that bike!

When we got paid every week, we put our money in a cigar box in the storeroom. We didn't tell Mr Wetstein this, figgerin' to spring it on him by handin' him the money all at once. I really wanted to see Mr W's face when we flashed the whole price of the bike at him! But of course we couldn't help but do a little braggin' to our chums after work. They was not happy at the idea of us gettin' a bike while they had to walk everywhere. Pretty soon, the whole of Rimson's Corners had heard about us an' our bike. I began to fear someone would buy that bike.

Sure 'nuff, one day I saw Mr Wetstein show the bike to a customer from over to Fosterville, a ways from us. I was petrified. I wanted to go tell the man that it was a lousy bike an' would prob'ly fall to pieces after a mile or two. I wanted to wait till they was both gone an' steal our bike to keep it out of the hands of that Philistine from Fosterville. But he didn't buy it. As he turned away, Mr. W. offered to pay the sales tax on the bike, yet the man still didn't want the bike.

This was the first time Wally an' me had heard of sales tax. Turns out, though there's no tax on groceries, there's a two an' a half percent sales tax on other stuff. We sold mostly groceries, so it had never come up. Mr. W. showed us the tax tables. With tax, the $40 bike was really $41.00, or $32.80, after our discount. Even worse, the chrome luggage rack was an "extra," another $3.00. Now the bike was up to $44, list, $35.26 net. Would we have it all before September? Prob'ly not.

We got real innerested in sellin' stuff to earn the thirty two dollars. We started pushin' like wildfire. We made every customer aware of every single thing he might need in the comin' week. This shifted the odds in our favor, but Mr. W. told us we was being "obnocshus little tverps." I'd never heard *obnocshus* before, but I knew it wasn't good. We had to back off a little. Still, sales was up, an' we soon had $16 in the cigar box.

And then sales went down, in spite of our best efforts. About a month after we'd started savin' for the bike, an A & P chain store opened in Fosterville. They took business away from Wetstein's, an' again it looked like we'd fall short of our goal.

Then an angel appeared out of nowhere. A dude in a snazzy suit and alligator shoes came into the store on a weekday morning an' asked for a pair of boots. Well, Mr. Wetstein wasn't in the store, so Wally looked at me an' I looked at Wally an' we went to town, showing this doofus all kinds of expensive stuff. He had no sales resistance at all. We sold him the boots, the best ones we had. Then I showed him a carbine, an' he said he'd take it. That led to eight boxes of cartridges, a cleanin' kit, an' a carryin' case. Wally talked him into buyin' a dozen boxes of good cigars an' a saddle, with stirrups an' saddle soap. We got his tab up to $168.25, with the tax, by far the biggest sale we'd ever rung up. Wally an' me was beside ourselves. We was extra polite, tryin' not to give even a tiny reason for the nincompoop to change his mind.

We boxed up his order an' set it on the counter. The dude pulled out a checkbook an' said, "I always pay by check. Of course you take checks, don't you?" He'd filled in the total an' signed the top sheet with a flourish while Wally an' me was still lookin' at each other. Yes, we did take checks, but that was when it was someone we knew. Should we tell this man we couldn't honor his check after he'd already writ it? Neither of us felt like doing that. We was afraid he'd leave the goods an' walk out in a huff.

The man put his check on the counter. Wally picked it up an' read it. A strange look took over his face. He handed the check to me. I read the name printed on the top of the check. It read: Montgomery Büthol.

There was only one 't', an' no 'e' at the end, an' two little dots over the 'u,' but it looked for all the world like 'butthole.'

We just about split a gut laughin'. Well, we would have laughed, but didn't dare, for fear of tickin' off this rich sucker name of Montgomery Butthole. We split a gut trying *not* to bust out laughin'. The man stayed deadpan an' didn't pay our titters an' sneaky looks at each other no never mind.

When Wally finally pulled himself together, he said, "We need to see your driver's license."

The man looked at us, eyes wide. "Do you boys think my check isn't any good?" He stood there in his new tweedy suit, with his gold watch chain festoonin' his silk vest an' his shiny shoes glintin' in the sunlight, the very epi-tome of offended wealth an' honesty. We shook our heads.

"'Course we don't," said Wally. "It's jus' that . . . " His voice faded off.

The man smiled down at us an' said, "Tell you what, my driver's license is back home in the glove box of my Dusenberg, but I have something much better than a driver's license; I have my *passport*."

We'd heard about passports, but had never seen one. We was more than a bit awed when the man pulls out a thin little green book an' waves it under our noses. Sure enough, there was his picture an' his name, Montgomery Phineas Büthol, 'midst a dozen official seals an' stamps an' signatures.

My throat ached from strainin' not to laugh. Right then, Wally an' me didn't even dare to look each other in the eye. After a long pause, Wally managed to say, "Thank you, Mr . . . Er, how do you say that?"

"We pronounce it 'Bew-thole," the man said. "It's a noble Swiss name. I'm directly related to Viscount Bew-thole, himself. It was he who gave me this thousand dollar Swiss watch." He brandished a great big gleamin' gold timepiece.

We put the check in the drawer an' helped Mr Bew-thole load his purchases in a rickety old wagon out front. He turned an' waved at us, grinnin' as he drove away, dust flyin' up from his wheels.

We was happy as clams for a minute. We had the bike money like it was in the bank. But then grimy-fingered doubt got to twiddlin' at our minds. The shabby wagon. The fact we'd never taken a check that size before, an' that Mr Wetstein almost always okayed any check over $5. Yes, we'd taken small checks from people we didn't know by simply writin' their driver's license number at the top of the check.

But we didn't think to do the same with a passport number. In fact, we hadn't even checked if the Bew-thole passport *had* a number.

By the time Mr. Wetstein came in that afternoon, we was full of doubt an' fear.

Wally took the bull by the horns. "Mr. Wetstein, there's somethin' you should know . . . "

Wetstein cocked his head an' squinted. "And vhat is dis somet'ing?" he growled.

Wally let go of the bull an' shoved it at me. "You tell him."

I foolishly thought good news might turn away any on-comin' disaster. "We sold $168 worth of goods to a new customer this mornin' while you was out."

For good news, this sure brought a lot of darkness to the face of Heinrich W. Wetstein. Terror, misery, an' wrath fought it out there. Misery won. He got right to the point. "Ach! Tell me you veren't taking a check for dis order."

"Uh . . . " I said.

"Er . . . " Wally said.

"Mein Gott! You *did* take a check." Mr Wetstein then swore. In German. I knew it was swearin', because there's nothin' like German if you want to swear. It leaves no doubt at all that you are bein' swored at. Standin' there, hearin' this cussin' an' seein' Mr Wetstein all red in the face, I felt like I could cringe like no one in the history of the world had ever cringed before. I wanted to cringe until I could peek out through my ribcage.

"Giff me de check!" Mr W. uttered. "Giff it to me!"

Wally hit the "No Sale" key an' drew the check from the cash register. When he shoved it in front of our boss, Wetstein looked at it, clutched his head, an' rocked back an' forth. "Maria in Himmel! You took a check from zumvun named Butthole!"

"He says it, 'Bew-thole," I said. Helpfully, I thought.

Wetstein looked at me. "Pinsel! Dummkopf! Esel! How could you do this thing? How could you trust a check written by a Montgomery Butthole?"

Wally was tongue-tied. I could only think to say, "Well, he *looked* just like a Montgomery Butthole. Bew-thole."

"He showed us his passport," Wally added.

I nodded. "I couldn't imagine anyone would say he was Montgomery Butthole, unless he really *was* Montgomery Butthole."

"And *I* can't imachine anyvun zaying he is Montgomery Butthole, *especially* if he is Montgomery Butthole," Wetstein groaned, his pained face less than a hand-breadth from mine, his breath reekin' of sauerkraut.

Reality struck us like a locomotive, and our hearts sank. Wally an' me didn't say anythin'. I just went an' got the cigar box. Weeping silently, we handed our money to Mr Wetstein. He counted it, said, "donkey shame," and wrote out a receipt with a balance due of only $100. He pointed at the sum and said, "I shall take dis balance out of your commish. Undershtood?"

We understood. That was the unhappiest day of my life at that point. It was also the day I decided never to steal from Mr. Wetstein again, the day I began to value honesty.

The Last Librarian

When they found him on that final winter morning, they downed their nuclear jack-hammers, removed their iridescent dymondyte helmets, and silently encircled him.

He stared upward, unseeing, at the ancient frescoes circling the rotunda high above. Twenty four volumes insulated his frail body from the night-cold marble floor: Bradbury beneath his snow-white head, Shakespeare beneath his feet. His blue-veined hands, now white in death, gently held *Wind In The Willows*.

The demolition foreman fumbled at his belt and turned off the fusion generator outside. Silence filled the library for the last time, a requiem unsung.

The disposal crew responded promptly to the foreman's call. They moved respectfully and efficiently, for they were all, save one, robots. Each performed his customary task. One metallomeric automaton carefully scanned the ID band on the librarian's wrist. Another took a DNA sample for positive identification. Finally, the mortician deployed the polymeric body-bag. Sapphire fluid oozed from the container, enveloped the deceased and the books beneath him, then hardened to a sky blue cocoon. Two robots placed the rigid cocoon on a gurney and trundled it outside to the Than-Van. The mortician left without a word.

The foreman reactivated the generator, and the building came down rapidly. Automated skip-loaders scooped books from the shelves to the shredder in minutes. Marble surrendered to the jackhammers after a brief struggle. Mahogany smoked and fell beneath the laborers' laser axes. Finally, all stood aside while the explosives went off, cracking the rotunda like an eggshell. Colorful confetti from the nineteenth century frescoes spattered briefly on the floor seconds before the entire dome collapsed. Soon the Ft. Powell library was but a memory.

Not that many remembered. Most citizens of Ft. Powell had never noticed the library. Those that had, seldom knew what the building was. Only a few elders could say, now, "That's where the library used to be. I remember the first time I went there . . . "

On the now-vacant property, the city would construct a suspect-monitoring facility, a building where blue-uniformed voyeurs scrutinized the glowing screens, day and night. Computers suggested in courteous, subdued monotones those screens most likely to need watching, where individuals previously designated as high-probability pre-criminals went about their daily routines.

But of course the library had been obsolete, unnecessary. Several months before, the city mothers had decreed it, "a wasta money."

The Mayor agreed, nodding sagely, "No longa cos'-effec'ive."

"Ol-timey shit," the city's website declared, "ol-fashion forest assination (sic)."

Shortly thereafter, the City Administrator, Omar Jones-Wong-Baker-Smith, sat in his bookless office on a bleak November day. The Librarian was shown in. Jones-Wong-and-so-on put his index finger below the Librarian's name on his computer screen. *Booker, yes, that's the man's name.* He smirked at the coincidence, then looked up. "Booker," he said, "as you know, the lib'ary is closin'."

Before the Librarian could part his lips to speak, the Administrator raised an emphatic hand. "No, don't go sayin' it. We heard all your argyments. The lib'ary has become a encumberance, a detirment to the very know-lidge you wanna perserve, and that's it. We've 'ranged for you to retire. You'll be quite comfor'ble, really, if you don't suddenly give up your famous fruggal lifestyle."

The Administrator smiled, trying not to glance at the Librarian's frayed cuffs and out-of-date attire, thinking: *the man actually still wears shoes instead of pneumo-sandals! Wherever does he find shoes these days? Or did he buy those things fifty years ago?*

"I'd hoped to find another library to work in," the Librarian said, looking down.

"Ours is the last one. I've looked it up on the Nexotron," Omar Jones-etc. replied, waving a finger towards his computer display.

"I know. I looked it up, too." The Librarian held up his wrist, encircled by an antiquated Interstellar Pondering Products computer.

"You are ol' enough to retire, and then some. Take a rest."

The Librarian smiled. "I'd rather work a while longer. I find work . . . absorbing."

"Well, if you really wanna work, there ain't no law again' it." Jones-etc. had looked *that* up, too. "You're a bright chap. I'll just say 'computers' and let it go at that."

"I've looked into it. Too much to learn, too little time."

"Then take a'van'age of that time to live a little. Play the games. Use your booze ration. Take the Zombinol tablets."

The Librarian shook his head.

Omar Jones-Wong-Baker-Smith stood up. "Well, thanks for comin' in, uh . . . " His eyes flicked furtively to the computer display. " . . . Booker. Your final pay will be credited to your account. Pension payments will begin promp'ly two weeks affer that." He held out his hand.

As the final shards of the library's dome were being robo-vac'd, elsewhere in the city stainless steel nozzles misted ether upon the Librarian's temporary shroud, dissolving it to slush in seconds. Robotic hands swept the books from beneath the body, diverting them to a disposal chute instead of the cremation slide. The books slid past the brief scrutiny of an eyebot, which determined them to be unrelated to its task and let them drop down another chute.

The trash container that was supposed to be at the other end of the chute was not there. Robots had commandeered it to move overflow victims of the city's gang wars to the crematoria. The books fell to the floor, unseen.

Janitor found the books there several days later, beneath the now-present container. He got down on his knees and retrieved them. Instinct told him to toss them into the dumpster where they belonged. But the books were attractive, despite their faint odor of ether. They were multi-colored, diverse, fascinating. He considered the matter for several minutes, then took all the books home in a bag.

The books lingered in the bag for several days as Janitor savored the presence in his life of *something different*. At last, some inner clock told him the time had come. He opened the bag and carefully took out the top book.

His life would never be the same.

Between the Universe

All the men must have dissolved today, washed away by the spring rain, Electra Fallon mused, looking around the nearly empty art museum.

It was just as well: she knew her hair, curly and blonde, almost, now hung down in dark, dripping stringlets. Her ratty brown raincoat and matching umbrella, also dripping, were not her normal chic attire. Sunday afternoon's expedition in search of cultured men was rained out. *Drat!*

She wandered from room to room for a while, then stood daydreaming by a window, watching the California rain splash down outside.

"That's the most awful thing I've ever seen!"

"Terrible, isn't it?"

Two passing women derailed Electra's train of thought. Hoping they weren't referring to her appearance, she looked around and located the object of their disgust.

A few feet away, a mauve and ecru lump about as big as a kitchen sink sat on a low platform. It was shapeless, except for various excrescences: rusty hubcaps, a broken toaster, old gloves, a lamp made from a decanter shaped like a telephone, and similar things. *It's truly awful,* Electra silently agreed. *I wonder what they call this hideous thing.* Under an illogical but powerful compulsion, she moved closer to read the card on the wall beside it. The card said:

BETWEEN THE UNIVERSE X
ACRYLICS ON PAPIER MACHÉ
AND OBJETS TROUVÉS
MISCHA WACOWSKY

Electra stepped back, slipped on a puddle, spun, regained her balance momentarily, then fell sideways, slowly, inexorably, directly on top of *Between the Universe X.*

"Oh, shitty-piss!" she cried as the sculpture crumpled beneath her. Electra disentangled herself and scrambled to her feet, horrified. Surveying the damage, she was relieved to see that the sculpture was regaining its shape, somewhat, with only an odd dozen new craters, tears, and dimples.

She looked around. There was no one in sight. *What luck!* she thought. Aside from her outcry and a muted *"whoompf!"* from *Between the Universe,* the accident had been silent and unseen. *With a little more luck,* she thought, *I can get out of here before anybody discovers the . . . the . . . corpse?*

But Electra hesitated. Running away seemed irresponsible. *I should do something,* she thought. *What if . . . ? What if I make just a few quick repairs? Then the thing won't look damaged, at all. With something this ugly, who'll ever notice an extra dent or two?*

She knelt down and reached in through the largest hole to poke the more obvious dimples back out. *Hurry, Electra,* she thought. *Almost done . . .*

"What in heaven's name are you doing? You vandal! You stop that at once!"

Electra looked up in horror. An immense woman was waddling towards her, brandishing a glistening, black Gucci umbrella. "I can explain," Electra began, planning to tell the woman there had been an unfortunate accident, that the damage was minor, and that it could be fixed in a jiffy.

But the woman's reddening face and uplifted umbrella quickly convinced Electra that explaining would be futile, possibly fatal. The woman's waddle, on the other hand, convinced Electra that Electra could outrun her. *To hell with Plan B; back to Plan A: run!*

She grabbed her umbrella and fled. Racing along deserted corridors, heart pounding with fright, she looked back as she neared a turning. Sure enough, the fat lady wasn't even in sight! Still checking behind her, Electra rejoiced. *Just another yard or two and I'll be safe! God, help me make . . .*

"*Oof!*"

Electra had caught only a brief glimpse of something grey out of the corner of an eye before the impact. She was already sitting on the floor before she identified the grey as a museum guard in full regalia.

"Hey, where ya goin' in such a big rush?" he asked, looking down at her.

I'll tell him I'm late for work, she thought. *"Pant, gasp, wheeze,"* she explained calmly, trying to stand.

"Huh?" said the guard.

"Gulp, wheeze, pant," she replied in her most persuasive manner.

"Whassa matter with ya? Ya okay?"

Did she hear heavy footsteps coming closer? Electra decided any further delay would be unwise, scrambled to her feet and bolted for the front door.

"Jussa minute, missy. I think ya better stick around a while." The guard clamped Electra's arm with a grip like a gorilla. "Ya been up ta something?"

"Wheeze, wheeze . . . " Electra shook her head.

"Then why ya runnin'?"

"Late . . . late for work," she managed at last.

"Oh." The guard's grip relaxed a little, to, perhaps, that of a baboon. "Where do ya work?"

"Parker's Department Store," Electra answered truthfully, afraid to lie again.

The gorilla grip returned. "Parker's is closed Sundays."

"I'm taking inventory," Electra lied.

"Oh." Baboon grip. The guard looked at his watch. "Getting sort of a late start, ain'tcha? It's after three." Gorilla.

"I'm on my lunch break."

"Oh." Baboon.

"Officer, stop that woman!" Electra's pursuer appeared at last, trundling around the corner, umbrella still waving.

Electra felt her horror grow as the guard now clamped down on her arm like the biggest gorilla that ever lived.

"What'd she do, lady?"

"I caught her vandalizing one of the works."

The guard's inner gorilla contorted his face with fury. "Come with me," he snarled..

He frog-marched Electra down long hallsways and across a foyer that led, eventually, to the curator's office. Electra's thoughts orbited between the pressure of the guard's clutching hand and amazement at how the formerly quiet museum was now simply jammed with people, all of them staring at her, nudging each other, and pointing in her direction. The umbrella-wielding Judas bounced proudly along behind. Electra felt her face redden with shame and a tear run down her cheek.

The nameplate on the curator's desk said: "Dr. Bella Basin, PhD." A very tall, muscular woman sat gazing out at the soggy knolls and dales of the museum landscaping.

"Doctor Basin, I think I caught the perp who's been damaging the art stuff . . . " the guard began.

"Aha!" The curator swiveled and leapt from her chair, eyes lit with wrath. "We've caught you at last, you filthy vandal!"

Electra cringed, hoping that this would somehow result in disappearing completely. No such luck.

"Oh. It's a woman," said Dr. Basin. "Not exactly what we were expecting, but good work anyway, Miller." She thumped the guard jovially on his shoulder, almost knocking him over.

"It was an accident . . . " Electra said.

"An accident? You've scrawled your initials all over our Warhols, and now you try to tell us it was an accident? You'll pay for these outrages."

"But I didn't write on anything . . . "

"Oh? What have you done now?"

"I caught her destroying one of the works in the west wing," interjected the fat lady, gesturing vigorously with her umbrella.

"Oh, no! The Wacowsky is in the west wing. How much damage has this trollop done? Bring the destroyer along, Miller. Handcuff her if she tries to escape." The amazon launched herself out the door ahead of them. "Judas" followed.

As they arrived at the "scene of the crime," Bella clutched her bosom. "Aaaa!" she yelled. "Aaaa!" she repeated, wrist to forehead. She turned on Electra. "You philistine! You saboteur! Look what you've done! First scribbling your initials on our Warhols, and now . . . this!"

"But I didn't write on your . . . holes, did you say?"

"Warhols, you ignoramus. Get the rest of her name, Miller, We already have her initials."

Electra meekly handed over her identification.

"Her driver's license says she's Electra Fallon, #305 Oak Drive," the guard said.

"Probably an alias. If her name is Electra Fallon, why did she write 'JC' on four of the Warhols?" Bella asked.

The guard leaned over Electra menacingly. "What about that, Fallon? Are you some kind of religious nut?"

"I think she's a communist," said the fat lady.

Bella glared at her. "You mean a fascist."

"Please," Electra said. "I didn't write on your Warhols, and I didn't mean to damage this . . . whatever it is. It was an accident. I slipped and fell on it. I was just trying to straighten it up a bit when this woman came along . . . "

The guard turned to the fat woman.

"Is that true, lady?"

"I—"

Bella cut her off.. "I'll handle this, Miller, if you don't mind. You get the witness's name and so forth. I'll take the sculpture and Ms. Fallon, as she calls herself today, back to the office."

"I still think she's a communist," the fat lady said.

"Shut up," said Bella.

Electra offered to help carry *Between the Universe* but was not allowed to touch it.

"You've done enough damage, you clumsy little twit," Bella said. "I hope you realize the seriousness of your situation, Ms. Fallon. Between the Wacowsky and the Warhols, you could be arrested for five counts of malicious destruction of property, a felony."

"But it was an accident–"

Bella ignored her. "The penalties for vandalism are very severe in this state."

"It was an acc–"

"You could be fined up to fifty thousand dollars."

"It was an–"

"And sentenced to six months in ja–"

"It was–"

"For each count."

"It–"

"Think of the scandal, Ms. Fallon." Bella scowled as they entered her office. "Sit!" she commanded.

Electra sat. "All right, I'll pay for the damage to the Wac . . . the wacky thingie."

Bella stopped scowling. "Wacowski. Now that that's settled, the work is probably damaged beyond repair. To replace it will cost twenty thousand dollars."

"*Twenty thousand dollars!?*"

"You heard me, Ms. Fallon."

"You paid twenty thousand dollars for this monstrosity?"

"This monstrosity, you uncultured boor, is a genuine Wacowsky, a work of the greatest *avant garde artiste* of the decade."

"But it's *ugly!*"

"Ugliness is in the eye of the beholder. The ignorant eye, in your case. That's the trouble with you bourgeoisie: you think you can tell what is beautiful and what isn't. Actually, you wouldn't recognize great art if you, well, fell on it." Bella smirked.

"But it's just a pile of junk covered with papier mache and some paint."

"That remark shows how abysmally ignorant you are of contemporary art." Bella rummaged around on her desk until she found a glossy brochure, which she handed to Electra. It was a price list of Wacowsky's artworks, with a photo on one page featuring a seedy-looking fellow standing beside *Between the Universe X* or its twin. The prices ranged from huge to astronomical.

"Mr. Wacowsky's work," continued Dr. Basin, "is acclaimed by all the important critics and is on display at all the best museums and galleries. He is considered the most relevant artist of the decade. Our *Between the Universe* is one of his finest works."

"Why does he call it '*Between the Universe Ex*'?"

"You're hopeless. The 'X' is a Roman numeral ten. This is the tenth *Between the Universe* he has made."

Electra waved the brochure. "You mean nine other suckers have paid twenty thousand dollars for one of these things?"

"*Twenty-two* other suck–" Bella frowned. "Twenty-two other art lovers. *Between the Universe* XXIII has recently been purchased for display at the Gagg & Humm Museum in New York."

"There are twenty-three? All just like this one?"

"Oh, yes. Wacowsky is a meticulous craftsman. There are small differences, of course, but each one is a recreation of *Between the*

Universe I. I believe he's switched to Renault hubcaps, though," she mused, looking far off. "Ours are Fow Vay."

Bella's mood seemed to have improved considerably. "Now," she said, "How do you propose to pay us the $20,000?"

"I haven't got $20,000."

"We could arrange for you to pay it off over a year . . . "

"It would take ten years to pay it off on my salary. I'm just an assistant window decorator at Parker's Department Store. Can't it be repaired? It doesn't look that badly damaged."

"Well . . . possibly." Bella frowned. "I suppose we shouldn't let this matter drag on for ten years. Perhaps the artist can restore it."

"Why can't you just let me fix it? All I have to do is pop up the dimples, patch these holes, and straighten out this funny-looking gizmo."

"That gizmo, as you call it, is Mr. Wacowsky's trademark, his neo-Dadaist phallic symbol!"

"Oh. I thought it looked like a pecker, but I wasn't going to say so. But why can't *I* fix it?"

"Ms. Fallon," Bella said coldly, "You are untrained in the aesthetics of transiency: If you profane this work with your untutored hands, it would totally lose the emotive chronological juxtaposition imparted to it by the artist. "

"The what?"

"*Between the Universe* is not merely a sculpture. It's a happening. Each component was added in a particular, meaningful chronological order. Only the artist himself can restore it to its original form without destroying his message, his expression of turmoil, his catharsis.."

"Catharsis? That sounds like . . . "

Bella frowned and held up a hand. "Please spare me any more vulgarity, Ms. Fallon. We'll send you the bill when we find out how much Mr. Wacowsky wants for the repair. Give me your phone number and you may go."

The bill arrived on Friday with a note from Dr. Basin urging prompt payment and hinting that she was still thinking of calling in the police. The bill was for five thousand dollars.

Electra fumed. "I could fix that damn thing myself with ten cents worth of glue. To hell with their 'emotive chronological juxtaposition!' I'd like to juxtapose my boot emotively to her chronological bum. If I can just get my hands on that piece of junk for fifteen minutes, nobody would ever be able to tell it was damaged."

Friday evening, the museum closed at eight p.m. The guards made a cursory check for dawdling visitors, then turned the building over to the janitorial staff. As soon as the cleaning crew dimmed the first floor lights and went upstairs, Electra Fallon crawled from behind a display cabinet.

Which office is Bella's? she wondered, trying to remember. *Oh, yeah, next to the restrooms. Here's the men's room, with the pointy triangular emblem. Next should be the ladies' room. Yes! Round emblem. Which means this next door is it. And here it is!* she exulted.

It was locked, of course. *Shitty-piss! Why did I assume it would be open?*

But Electra knew you could open a door with a plastic card. She'd never done it, but she'd seen it often on television. She fumbled in her purse for her Moonbeam's Coffee gift card and forced it between the jamb and the door. After considerable effort, she worked it down to the latch. The latch moved a tiny bit. She pushed harder. Maybe if she angled the card a little . . .

The card popped out of her fingers and disappeared through the crack. *Damn! I've still got five dollars left on that card.* Now I *have* to get into Bella's office.

She reached into her purse again and took out her Discount Mounties credit card. She shoved it into the crack, and wiggled it carefully down to the latch. Carefully. Carefully . . .

Suddenly, she heard voices echoing from the distant foyer. Bella Basin said, "Oh, Mr. Wacowsky, I was so happy to hear you were going to be in Los Angeles for the weekend."

Oh, jeesh, they're coming! Electra jerked her credit card from the door and looked for a way out. She tried the restroom doors. Both were locked. Could she make it to the far end of this corridor before Bella and Wackowsky arrived? Maybe not.

Electra ran back to Bella Basin's door and jabbed at the latch with the credit card. The voices were only one corridor away, now.

Electra prayed and gave the card a push. The door opened, just like it was supposed to. *Yee-haa!* She ran inside and closed the door.

It was dark in Bella's office. Electra automatically reached for the light switch before realizing that would give her away. She dropped the credit card safely into her purse, wondering, *How the hell do I get out of here?*

She dashed to the window. Beneath it on a table sat *Between the Universe*, gleaming ecru and mauve in the light of the setting moon.

Electra heard Bella gush from the corridor outside: "It's so nice to see you again, Mr. Wacowsky."

"Yeah, ain't it?" a man said fuzzily. "*Urrrp.* Call me 'Mike.' When do I get the thou?"

Wacowsky must be high as a kite. Electra was halfway out the window when she heard Bella say: "I'll pay you tonight, as soon as you fix it."

He's going to fix the sculpture right now! For $1,000! And then she'll gouge me for the full $5,000. Unless . . .

Electra wrestled *Between the Universe* out the window and jogged away into the night, congratulating herself on her quick thinking.

Behind her, the office lit up, and Bella's scream soon broke the stillness. Seconds later, floodlights started coming on all around the museum, and it sank in that Electra was actually stealing *Between the Universe.*

Dang! It seemed like such a brilliant idea on the spur of the moment, but if I get caught with this thing, I'll be arrested for burglary. I've got to get rid of it now and get out of here! So much for quick thinking.

Electra was about to drop her burden and kiss five thousand dollars goodbye, when she saw a dilapidated garden shed deep in shadowy bushes and all overgrown with wisteria. *Perfect!* she thought. *If I can hide the sculpture here, I can sneak back tomorrow, after Wacky Man leaves, and fix it. Then I can just phone Bella and tell her where to find it.*

She slid the doors open. The shed evidently wasn't used much. The faint illumination of the flood lights revealed that it held only spiderwebs, a shovel, and several dozen bags of horse manure. Electra hid *Between the Universe* behind the bags, closed the doors and crept away, keeping in the shadows and listening for sirens.

She was home by 9:15 and fell onto her sofa, exhausted. Suddenly, her eyes opened wide. *Hell! I forgot my Moonbeam's gift card. Oh, well, no big deal. If all goes well, I'll have saved myself four thousand nine hundred and ninety five dollars.* She closed her eyes.

At 9:20, Electra's cell phone rang. She woke up enough to fumble around in her purse for it. She couldn't find the phone. *What's this? Oh, it's my Moonbeam's gift card. I didn't leave it behind, after all. Goodie.* She dumped the contents of her purse onto the sofa and snatched up the phone.

"Hullo?" she said.

"You little worm!" It was Bella. She was very upset.

"What's the matter, Dr. Basin?"

"You know what's the matter, you thief! You stole our Wacowsky."

"What makes you think I stole it? Maybe some art lover took it."

"For one thing, you knew where it was."

"Oh? Where was that?"

"In my office, of course."

"But I don't have a key to your office."

"Fallon," Bella said calmly.

"Yes?"

"Surely you've seen how burglars can use a plastic card to jimmy open a door, haven't you?"

I don't like the sound of this at all, Electra decided. "No, I don't know anything about that."

"Well, that's too bad," Bella boomed, "because if you did, you'd know they don't leave a Discount Mountie credit card behind with their name embossed on it."

There were long seconds of silence as Electra realized which card she'd grabbed first from her purse in the dimly lit museum corridor. *Oopsie.*

"Oh, is that where that thing went to? I've been looking all over for it. I must have dropped it Sunday when I was in your office . . . "

"Fallon, you're fooling no one. I know you took the Wacowsky."

"You can't prove that I did."

"But we have enough proof to get you arrested on suspicion. Think how that will look down at Parker's Department Store.

"Oh."

"Fallon, I'm busy tonight, but if that sculpture isn't back here before closing time tomorrow, eight p.m., I'm calling the police."

"If you're so sure I stole it, why haven't you called them already?"

"I have other plans. Besides, I detest policemen. They're all fascists." Bella hung up.

Electra sighed wearily and got dressed.

Twenty minutes later she was back at the shed, brushing particles of manure off the sculpture. She picked it up and trudged over a hill toward the darkened museum, grateful that the moon was down and the floodlights extinguished. No one could see her. She could just put this albatross on the front steps unobserved and then get a good night's sleep at a cost of only $5,000. It almost seemed worth it.

KERSPLOOSH!

"*Aieeee!*" In the darkness, Electra had walked over the edge of a bluff and was now hip-deep in an ornamental pond. *Between the Universe,* torn from her hands, had disappeared into the cold, dark waters with a single disconsolate *glub.* Soon Electra was up to her navel in the deepest water, feeling around with both hands and feet.

"Oh, no! Oh, geez! Where is it?" she cried. She probed in all directions and found nothing. "It must have floated off somewhere. Dang! What's this?"

"This" was a loose round object like a salad bowl. Electra held it up. In the faint light, she could just make out: "VW." An ominous discovery.

"Oh, hell!" She reached down and felt beneath her feet. There was something . . .

She brought up her hand and found she was clutching a soggy hunk of papier mache with a neo-Dadaist pork stick attached. Electra had been standing directly atop *Between the Universe* for some time. There was nothing left of the sculpture but a lumpy mass and assorted flotsam and jetsam. It was a total loss. Electra gave herself permission to cry.

But somehow tears were inadequate. Electra swore instead. It made her feel much better and she continued with increasing enthusiasm.

"I am not going to pay a frogging nickel for this frogging piece of frogging junk!" she said finally.

Early the next morning, Electra drove to an art supply store. On the way home, she stopped at a junk yard and a costume rental shop.

Later that afternoon, a large mauve and ecru lump was drying under a heat lamp on Electra's kitchen table. It was a fair replica of *Between the Universe X*: the hubcaps and all the larger artifacts had been salvaged from the pond the night before. The rest of it closely matched the photo in the brochure Bella had given Electra.

Near dusk, a slightly-built, bearded man in a delivery service uniform entered the back door of the museum, wheeling a large parcel on a hand truck. "Package for Dr. Basin," he told the guard hoarsely.

"Okay, just leave it here."

"Oh, no," said the bearded one, "She's supposed to sign for it personally." He brandished a clip board.

"The curator's office is straight ahead, then left at the dead people, right at the Renaissance stuff, and left again at the naughty Greek crockery. Ya can't miss it."

But the delivery man didn't turn right at the Renaissance stuff. He turned left and trundled quickly down a deserted corridor to the empty platform by the window.

In a trice, *Between the Universe X-1* stood in sparkling mauve-and-ecru glory on the platform. The "delivery man" stuffed the empty carton behind the sarcophagus, and waved his clip board at the guard on his way out.

The phone rang that night. Electra picked it up. "Hullo?"

"Very clever, Fallon, very clever. But your little forgery didn't fool me for an instant!"

"What little forgery, Bella?"

"Don't play dumb with me, you . . . you trollop! My patience is exhausted. I'm calling in the police."

"I wouldn't do that if I were you, Bella."

"And why shouldn't I?"

"Because I will sue you for extortion and false arrest. And maybe for personal injury. I think I hurt my back when I fell on your neo-Dadaist whangdoodle. We're talking a million dollars, here, maybe two."

"Don't be ridiculous. You've stolen our Wacowsky."

"I am prepared to swear in court that I don't have your Whackoffsky and that I never took it from the museum grounds in the first place. You can search for it wherever and whenever you like."

"And I am prepared to testify that the amateurish imitation now on display is not *Between the Universe X*."

"What evidence do you have?"

"The very best evidence: the word of the artist himself."

"Merely an opinion. One belch out of him and the court will laugh that lush right off the stand. What else have you got?" Electra asked.

"We have a photo. In the brochure."

"Which photo? The one of *Between the Universe I*? Or VIII? Or maybe XIX? The photo that's two inches square and sort of fuzzy? It will never stand up in court."

Bella paused, then said, "We won't need photos. The court will certainly accept the word of two experts over your own uneducated assertions."

"You're forgetting one thing. The jury will be twits. Bourgeoisie. Uncultured boors. What else did you call me? Oh, yes, ignoramuses. Do you seriously think that a panel of bourgeoisie will believe there's any real difference between one pile of junk and any of twenty-two just like it?

"Picture this, Bella. You're in court and your attorney shows the jury *Between the Universe* for the first time. What are the odds that at least one of those twelve philistines on the jury will look at that pile of mauve crap and think it's excruciatingly funny? Once he starts laughing, the whole courtroom will join in."

There was silence at the other end of the line.

"Why take a chance on getting sued? Think of the scandal! Think of the two million you might lose! If you keep quiet, no one will ever know that your *Between the Universe* might not be the real thing."

"Wacowsky knows."

"Buy him a bottle of scotch."

"*You* buy him a bottle of scotch!"

"All right, I will."

"And you surely won't be stupid enough to tell anyone else, will you?"

"Of course not. Not if you'll agree to drop the entire matter."

"Oh, very well. I give up." Bella sighed wearily. "Just do me one favor, Fallon."

"What?"

"Please, please, don't ever let me see you in my museum again."

"That's fine with me, Bella. I've got better things to do, much better things, than wandering around your junk collection." Electra hung up.

"That's the most atrocious thing I've ever seen."

"Yes, revolting, isn't it?"

Milton Conner's reverie was broken by the exclamations of disgust. He turned from his view of the snow falling on Philadelphia and looked over at the sculpture beside the window.

It was amorphous, almost, and chartreuse and orange, more or less, with assorted protuberances: old bottles, light bulbs, part of a carburetor, and a clock.

"Yuck! " Milton thought. Still, he read the card on the wall. It said:

DRUMS ALONG LAKE NERNEY XVII
PAPIER MACHE, OBJETS TROUVÉS,
& ACRYLICS
ELECTRA FALLON

The Search for Baba Gondahara-Ji

My search began early in life. Even when I was very young, I had a sense that there was something I had not been told, something important that everybody else in the world knew. I annoyed my parents by asking questions constantly, hoping that their answers would fill the empty part of my mind and bring serenity. School provided me with more questions than answers. Questions like "Why is it okay for the bigger kids to beat me up at recess? Why is Sister Hemorrhoida mean to all the boys and nice to all the girls?

In college, though, I joined this cult called "Technosophy." It seemed to have a lot of answers, but it turned out to be more science fiction than religion. They had this belief system that . . . oh, never mind. It worked for some people, not for me.

Over the years that followed, I imagined that the answer lay among earthly pursuits. Wine, women, and song, not necessarily in that order. A variety of unsuitable relationships occurred, in which perplexed women tried to answer my unspoken questions, which were usually posed in the form of untenable situations for them to solve. Sooner or later, they left. If they didn't, I did.

I was raised by non-drinking parents and never really drank seriously until well into my twenties. My first drink was an incredible experience. It didn't gave me answers; it just made me forget the questions. Ultimately, I learned the hard way that alcohol giveth and alcohol taketh away. The first thing it tooketh away was my ability to tell what it was doing to me. I lost control over it in a few weeks.

A serious auto accident ended my drinking. It also, dipso facto, ended my driving. I became healthy, especially my leg muscles, as I walked off the mental fuzziness of the previous year. I had a lot of interesting conversations with people on the bus. The benefits of not having a driver's license go on and on.

When I got my license back, I tried race cars, motorcycles, tennis, and jogging. And soccer and gambling, buying stocks high and selling low, and working sixteen hour days.

Then there were computers. Surely devices so good at answering the most complex questions known to human science could provide me with the simple answers I sought. But no; they merely allowed me to ask bigger questions and receive fast, complex answers whose irrelevance took years to grasp. The time I saved using a computer was quickly eaten up on hold with Microflob and Zymandec tech support.

Ultimately, I decided computers were only expensive toys. I threw my last one into the sea as habitat for small fish.

I'd abandoned my early religious upbringing when it failed to give me fast answers. Now, all the fast, wrong answers of past years made me more tolerant of slowly-reached answers. I resumed my spiritual quest.

After several years of this church and that church and a mosque or synagogue or two, I abandoned conventional religion. I decided that most religion is spirituality designed by committee, ultimately more concerned with corporate survival than spiritual growth. In a sincere sort of way, of course.

I got into meditation of various sorts, always feeling that enlightenment was just one experience away, that spirituality would surely arrive in a flash of light. It never did, quite. Oh, I got something out of it, but I found that spirituality was a moving target. As soon as I told myself *I've got it!* I didn't have it anymore. Frustrating.

Eventually, I undertook a pilgrimage. It took me to many strange places in search of truth: Florida, Maine, Montana, Mexico, Oregon, Georgia, and other places I've forgotten. I learned a little here and a little there from various gurus and teachers. Then I'd move on in search of a better teacher.

Finally, my quest led me to a tiny and remote mountain village, high above San Bernardino. There I met a seeker of truth named Zamadusapendalama. Zamadusapendalama, hereinafter referred to simply as Zamadusapendala, was originally from Peoria. Born "Jason Schwartz," he had spent nine years, count 'em, nine years meditating in India under the tutelage of some Indian dude who supposedly had been enlightened by another famous Indian dude I'd never heard of, who, in turn, had been taught by another tutel-dude whose name I actually recognized, Baba Gondahara-Ji.

Anyway, this Zamadusapenda guy had a little ashram near Big Bear, and he could do stuff. Amazing stuff. He held both my hands while I meditated and told me about myself. Somehow, he knew about the alcohol, the auto accident, the women. He said he could read all this in my "aura."

He could sense people's presence. He'd say "Rebecca is coming." Sure enough, she'd show up about a minute later. He could tell time without a watch. He didn't even own a wristwatch. He'd fold his arms and roll his eyes upward, then say something like, "It is a half before the hour of two." He was right every time, almost to the minute.

I took this as proof of his deep spirituality. I wanted to learn how to do all these nifty things. I wanted him to teach it all to me. Zamadusapen gave me a list of things I had to do to become "enlightened." Mostly, I had to do tasks for him: fix him breakfast, give him donations for food, sell copies of his books, and so on. He had four other adherents, three guys and a gal, who had to call him "Babu," and do chores for him in exchange for meditation lessons.

I got tired of this right away, but kept on going, hoping to learn what I needed to know. The others had been around for a long time and seemed pretty dedicated. We had to get up before dawn, then work and pray and meditate until after midnight. There was not a lot of sleep or food at Zamadusa's.

Still, I was impressed with what Zamadusa could do. The guy could read my mind, I swear he could. He told me one morning: "You are thinking of going away. I cannot stop you." I was so impressed, I decided to stay.

After several months of this, though, I was still unenlightened. I found out by sheer accident that Zamadusa was having Rebecca practice horizontal yoga positions in bed with him after everybody else had flopped on their futons from fatigue. I also found out that when he was supposedly meditating privately in his yurt, he was actually taking naps, snoring softly while everybody else was working their tails off, dizzy from lack of sleep.

I was getting desperate, by this point. I'd learned over the years that there was something to all this devotion stuff, meditation, call it what you will. I also knew I was getting nowhere. I finally asked Zamadusa to give me a letter of introduction to the guy in India who had taught him. Well, of course, Zamadusa told me that the guy who'd been his "spirit guide" had gone away somewhere, was unavailable, possibly even "ascended." (That means dead in woo-woo talk.)

I eventually realized that the guy who'd guided Zamadudu might or might not be unavailable, but that still left the next guy up the chain, Om Babalu. One night, Zamadudu had been showing us photos and stuff of his guru and there among the clippings was a pamphlet about "Om Babalu," the guy who'd taught his guru. Zamadudu quickly shoved it under the stack, but I'd taken it in at a glance, including the name of the place in India where he hung out, Pondicherry.

I left that same night. I already had a passport and enough money to buy a ticket to India. A week later, I was there, in Bombay. Actually, there is no Bombay, despite what you've heard. It's actually called Mumbai. Close enough. Bollywood should now be called "Mollywood."

India is quite a place. It doesn't all smell like incense, I can tell you! I stayed one night in a hotel, then went to the train station and asked where to get a train to Pondicherry. I found several people who spoke English, or thought they did. I was pretty sure I understood the hand gestures and the head wagging, and was soon on an antique train chugging across the country. I'd describe the trip in detail, but it's not really relevant. Go see it for yourself. It's pretty exotic.

I was dead tired by the time the train got in, a day or two later. Then the fun began. I discovered that, despite being on a train, I was lost. How could this be? Well, there are four Pondicherrys, in India. They are not a city, not even a state. They're a collection of former French colonies strewn across southern India like friggin' Yahtzee dice on a table, only one of the dice is missing. I was in the wrong piece of Pondicherry.

It took me a week to track down Om Babalu in Karaikal, a piece of Pondicherry south of the one I'd been sent to. I was running low on money, by then. To cut to the chase, Om Babalu had a huge ashram ten miles outside Karaikal. A walled fortress, is what it was. People were lined up halfway to town to apply for admission. I talked to some sort of clerk who looked me (and my wallet) over and then made it clear in very bad English that I had just two chances of getting taken on as a student there: slim and none.

I was devastated, but I've become tenacious over the years. I decided to hunt up the guy who'd taught the guy who'd taught the guy who'd taught Zamadudu, Baba Gondahara-Ji, himself. I asked around Karaikal and heard he was in a monastery in the Himilayas, perched on the slopes of a peak called K-652. There was a local name for it, but it was too complicated to remember. K-652 was clear at the other end of India.

It took two weeks to get there. I took a train north to New Delhi, then caught another train north to a town below the Himalayas. From there I'd planned to take a bus to the village nearest the monastery. Unfortunately, by then I'd almost run out of money and decided to save rupees by buying a rusty bicycle. I pedaled out in the right direction, more or less. Bicycles work better than anything else in India. They always leave on time. They get there on time, unless you're going uphill. Or you get a flat.

I figured had just enough rupees and tire patch material to make it to the monastery. After that, I'd have to beg my way back to the States, unless they let me stay at the monastery. It was a lot farther than I'd thought. I hadn't had much to eat in two or three days. I broke a chain, skidded off the road and took an unscheduled detour down the side of a small mountain. I finally dragged my ass into the monastery, bruised, torn, starved, sunburned, flea-bitten, dehydrated, hauling a bicycle with two flat tires and a broken chain.

A monk opened the gate and helped me in. He wanted me to leave the bicycle outside, but I had a death-grip on the handlebars. It was my only way back home, which was pretty much downhill from the monastery. No chain required, mostly.

Well, they fed me and patched me up. When I was able to stand again, they told me the bad news: Baba Gondahara-Ji had left many days before, headed to a little meditation hut several miles further up the mountain. The monks told me he was only going to stay there another day or two and then would be leaving before winter for some unknown destination. They gave me some old pieces of scrap tires to patch my bicycle, and I left the monastery, walking my bike up the side of K-652 to save the tires for the return trip.

As the monastery gate closed behind me, snow started to fall. The sub-arctic air burned my lungs. I was not in very good shape, and I staggered the last mile, barely making it to the little hut with icicles on my beard and in my eyebrows. I fell beside the door and knocked feebly.

After a long time, the door opened a crack and I could smell curry and incense wafting out into the snowy air.

"Yes?"

"Baba Gondahara-Ji?"

"Yes? Vhat you are vanting?"

"I seek enlightenment."

"Ah. That. Come in, Hopgrasser."

Baba Gondahara-Ji was a little guy, not even 5 feet tall. He was very old, but not the least bit feeble. He sat me down and put blankets around me. He fed me something hot; I don't know what it was. I was exhausted, but I sensed a power about him, something indescribable. He *knew*. He had answers. I could feel it and see it in his eyes.

When I'd rested a little, he talked with me. He asked me questions, but didn't let me ramble. After a half hour of this, he started to tell me things, the real stuff. He told me wonderful thoughts, rules for living, the secrets that made every part of life seem to fit together into an integrated whole. Even parts of Technosophy. I don't remember which parts.

Oh, and he told me about Braille watches, for some reason. Yes, it all made sense, but I was too tired to take it in. I was sleepy, exhausted from the trip, weak from my ordeal and months of poor diet in Zamadudu's ashram. I kept fading in and out. Dreams flitted through my mind, even as I was listening to Baba Gondahara-Ji's wonderful teaching.

I wanted to write it all down, but I had no paper or pen. It all seemed like part of a dream. Finally, I slumped forward with my head on the table.

I woke some time later, a pillow under my head. Baba Gondahara-Ji was dressed for travel, wearing some sort of hooded robe, an embroidered over-garment, and heavy boots on his feet. "I must be going, little pilgrim. I hope you are remembering vhat I said."

"I . . . no! I can't remember anything. Please, tell it all to me again!"

He shook his head. "Alas, pilgrim friend, I must go. The caravan is outside, vaiting for me. I have far to go and must be on my vay before the storm is vorsening. You may stay here; the monks vill be helping you back to the monastery in a day or two . . . maybe three."

I was devastated. To come all this way, to meet the one who really did have answers, then lose it all. "Please, I'll come with you." I tried to get up, but my legs wouldn't hold me. I slumped back down.

"You are not vell enough to travel. You are too veak! Rest, little pilgrim."

"Where are you going? I'll catch up with you in a few days, when I'm stronger."

"I am going someplace you cannot go. Do not ask vhere. It is a secret, and I cannot possibly be telling you." He turned and started out the door. Snow swirled into the little hut.

"But all the teaching . . . it's fading from my mind . . . I must find you again."

He looked back at me. "Oh, no, no, little pilgrim. You must not be seeking me again on this physical plane. You must be saving your energy. No more vandering from place to place. You can achieve vunness vith me in another vay, in the vibrations that are omnipresent." He arced his hands high and wiggled all his fingers. "You understanding?"

"I should seek you in the spirit?" I pointed to my heart.

He smiled and raised a finger, his eyes twinkling. "Oh, no, no, Hopgrasser! Vorld Vide Veb! Babagondaharaji dot net." Then he closed the door and was gone. A few snowflakes melted on the floor behind him.

Excerpt: *Sherlock and the Twelve Apostles* (coming in 2020)

I heard footsteps slowly ascending the stairs. "Hark, Watson!" said Holmes. "Who would this be?"

"I was just thinking of retiring."

"Wait a bit, Watson. Let's see what our visitor wants." Holmes took a puff on his pipe and looked towards the door. "He's an elderly clergyman, and he very likely wishes to borrow money."

"Shall I tell him to go away, then?" I must confess I was more interested in sleep than mystery.

"No, no, Watson. He would like to consult us on a disturbing or awkward matter. Let him in, would you?"

I opened the door and startled an elderly man in a clerical collar, his fist already raised to knock. "Are you Mr. Sherlock Holmes?" he asked. His voice was deep and resonant, far more stentorian than I'd expected from such an elderly man.

"I'm Dr. John Watson. Who shall I say is calling?"

"I'm Fr. Francis Habakkuk of St. Rupert's Church," he said, "and I'm dreadfully embarrassed to ask, but could I prevail upon your Christian charity to borrow sixpence? I'm afraid I'm short on the cab fare."

I found the necessary coin and handed it to him. As he slowly descended the stairs, I turned to Holmes. "Once again, you've got me almost completely baffled. How did you know he'd be a needy cleric? Elementary, I presume, but I still must hear it."

❦

Excerpt: *The Perils of Tenirax, Mad Poet of Zaragoza* (coming 2019)

A voice called out, full of morning enthusiasm, "Wakey-wakey!" Tenirax was not of that persuasion, preferring to greet the dawn only once it was well to the west of him.

¿Who is this lout that wakes a man at such an ungodly time of day, he wondered. *There seems to be an echo, so I must be home in my little hideaway beneath the ruined chapel. But how did this rude oaf get in?*

"You're in the dungeon," a little voice said in his mind.

Suddenly remembering where he was, and why, Tenirax sat upright and opened his eyes to the horror that awaited him. There, beside the rack, was Bungorolo, already stripped to the waist and leather-aproned.

The torturer was raking hot coals from an iron scuttle into a large brazier beside the rack, humming a simple tune as he did so. He looked at Tenirax "Come! You must join me." Bungorolo opened the cell door and helped the poet to his feet.

"I'd rather stay in here, if you don't mind." Tenirax shivered.

"Nonsense. It's much warmer out here. Have a seat. Warm yourself." The torturer indicated the rack and brazier.

Tenirax hobbled over to the rack and cautiously sat on the edge, expecting at any moment to be grabbed and forcibly strapped in place. He noted Bungorolo's beefy arms, thicker than his own thighs, and estimated how many seconds lay between him and profound agony. Perhaps as few as ten, he thought.

Bungorolo reached out a hand, and Tenirax recoiled in utmost fear. But Bungorolo merely bent down and pulled a grille from beneath the rack, then placed it across the brazier, followed by a small pan. Soon, the aroma of frying eggs and a bit of meat met Tenirax's nose.

"Want some?" the torturer asked.

"Not hungry," was all Tenirax could manage to say.

☙

Excerpt: *Sail Away on My Silver Dream* (2019) Chapter 1: Clouds

The first scary thing happened on Saturday, a week before school started. It was really hot that day. I was in the back yard, using the weed trimmer and getting all sweaty and covered with shredded grass. Mom had her long, brown hair done up in a bandana and was wearing her grubby jeans, cutting roses beside the garden shed. I saw her straighten up, and then she dropped her clippers and just stood there like a statue. Something was wrong with the way she was standing. I stopped what I was doing and wondered, *What's the matter with Mom?*

❦

Excerpt: *In the Mouth of the Lion* (2016)

The German spoke. "Dr. Jung, I come on the behalf of my employer, Mr. Wolff, who desperately needs the kind of healing you specialize in."

Jung waved the idea away. "My practice is closed. I am taking no new clients . . . "

The man became less confident. "Perhaps if you heard some of the details—"

Jung was tempted to ask him to explain, but fear overruled his curiosity. "No, no. I am not interested."

"Please, Herr Dr. Jung. Mr. Wolff has met you and wants you in particular."

"We have met? I don't recall a 'Mr. Wolff.' Who is this Mr. Wolff?"

The German leaned back and folded his arms across his chest. "Adolf Hitler."

❦

Excerpt: *Something Wicked in Ichekaw* (2019)

Sheriff Del Singletary looked across at the Regulator clock on the wall above the gun rack. The brass pendulum was slowly ticking off the last minute before the hour hand touched six. Singletary drew his booted feet off the big oak desk, stood, and rolled up his revolver in its leather gun belt before shoving it into the bottom drawer. He put on his heavy, crimson-and-black checkered hunting jacket and his black Stetson, then bent down by the big front window to turn the sign to CLOSED. "Well, that's enough shit for one day," he said, standing up and stretching to his full six foot four.

A red pickup truck screeched to a halt outside. As it rocked back on its springs, Sheriff Singletary saw a flash. A hole appeared in the window in front of him, and something struck him in the chest like an invisible fist. He staggered, steadied himself, then lunged toward the gun rack, reaching for the nearest lever action Winchester. He could hear the window shatter and more shots being fired, but ignored everything except the pain in his chest and the nearest rifle. As blackness engulfed him, Singletary fell to the gritty, bare wooden floor, dead before the last shard fell from the window pane.

❧

Excerpt: *Out Brief Candelle* (2019)

BOOM! BOOM! BOOM! Far away, a fist pounded on a door. *An oaken door*, Quynt Quayne thought. *Heavy, 'tis, with sturdy, black-iron hinges . . .*

Hoy! 'Tis my door, he thought, finally waking. *That is someone downstairs at my own door.* He opened his eyes and looked towards the clock at the foot of his sleeping cubicle. A phosphorescent "III" glowed faintly through the opening in the clock face. *Three of the clock. 'Tis the middle of the flacking night. They must want me to snuff someone. By the four kings, I really need to find better work.*

❧

Biography

J Guenther, B.S., M.S., University of Southern California, has written 22 stage plays, three computer books, four magazine articles, 50 short stories, five novels and 111 poems. His three-act play *Midnight in the Temple of Isis* and many shorter works for the stage have been performed from Los Angeles to Santa Barbara. *Prisoner of Suggins Holler* was a prize winner in Elite Theatre Company's 2010 One-Act Play Contest. His *Sorcerer of Deathbird Mountain*, was nominated for best novel, 2005 Santa Barbara Writers Conference.

A Final Note

We hope you've enjoyed *Tales For a Blue Moon*. It was fun to write these stories. But having written a book is more fun than writing it. And one of the very best parts of having written a book is hearing from people who enjoyed it! Please let leave a comment at: https://jguentherauthor.wordpress.com/

Better than that, even, is when readers tell other people they liked our book, either by word of mouth or in the form of a review on their favorite book discussion website. Please be one of our angels and post a review. It doesn't have to be very long.

❧